MW00791976

THE ANVILS

Kevin Kilroy

SPUYTEN DUYVIL
New York City

© 2024 Kevin Kilroy

ISBN 978-1-963908-01-5

Library of Congress Control Number: 2024939975

As soon as you trust yourself, you will know how to live.
If not, you'll sit forever, gluing things together
Cooking up a stew from other's scraps
Blowing on a miserable fire
Made from your heap of dying ash.
Let apes and children praise your art
If their admiration's to your taste
But you'll never speak from heart to heart
Unless it rises up from your heart's space.

Johann Wolfgang von Goethe, *Faust*

CHAPTER ONE

The Anvil was an old bar around the corner from where we lived when our kids were young. People told me Chicago's writers hung out there, but when I asked who, the names I heard were never anyone I'd read, so I avoided it for a long while.

When I got laid off from my teaching position at the arts college and sought to hammer out my life by doubling down on my commitment to novels, I decided to see for myself. The regulars at The Anvil were older professional-types. Newsdesk editors, communications managers, journeyman copywriters. They wrote canned tuna, not Moby-Dick. Still I began to drink there most nights, waiting for one or the other to appear.

I'd walk in, take a seat, nod to Jeremiah and stare at his long beard as he poured me a beer. Waiting for the talk to start flowing, I'd watch the scene in the silvered-glass mirror that ran the stretch of the bar, hoping to catch a clue. It was like taking in a Chinatown storefront filled with those Lucky Cats waving their paws, one golden arm on each of us bringing the pint up to the mouth and back to the coaster. Once we had a couple, the silence would be interrupted as arms wiped the wet from beards and the faces began to speak.

—They cut the balls off my headline again.

—Who?

—Jimmy.

—Fuck Jimmy.

—One thing I know I do better than anyone in that office is cobble together a headline that screams *read me.*

—Is that the editor they hired away from Leo Burnett?

—That fella has taken his share of headlines if you know what I'm saying.

—Listen to this epiphany I had today.

—Don't go telling us you joined the circus again, Barry.

—The Red Line stalled out after the Wilson Stop. For 45 minutes I sat squeezed in next to a homeless piece of shit. All over his pants, literally. I closed my eyes, right, but I didn't fall asleep—like I was soaring further and deeper. Everything I ever wanted to know—the meaning of life, the location of the holy grail, every last line of Homer's *Margites*—and right then as my soul was dancing through the all-knowing realm, this woman standing above me spewed her lunch all over my lap.

—No!?

—In the vomit across my book it was as if she had swallowed one meatball whole. Round, rancid and crenulated by its passage.

—Barry's such a fucking wordsmith.

—Someone buy me a beer, I can still fucking smell it.

—How are you not giving up your seat to the lady in the first place?

—Sucks to stand and read.

—You've gotta stop riding the clown cars to work, Barry.

—Put that in your novel.

—In my drawer for years now, may it rest in peace.

—What were you reading?

—The kid speaks! Huzzah!

—*The Lazarus Project.*

—Do you know Hemon?

—That stuff Barry reads is garbage, kid. You know who used to drink here?

—Who?

—Scott Turow, that's who.

—I've never read him.

The Anvil had been there almost as long as the city itself and the mirror and bar were original. I tried to sit in front of a portion that had not given way to the tarnished clouds winnowing across the surface. But I was also fascinated by the darkened and distorted crystalline webs sparkling before the bar flies' eyes. The decades of German and Irish Catholic faces staring into the silvered glass left an uncrackable layer of compunction which kept

9

me from breaking through. I had a hunch that something I needed was waiting on the other side, and I spent many nights looking within the clouds for a way forward.

On the best nights some unexpected story unwound, a great memory from the days of running with the horses, and everyone's faces grew warm and smiled. But most nights the voices simply excavated the bore began long ago, chastising all those selfish cusses trampled underfoot, and toasting men, who like themselves, had looked only as far as the mirror's imperfections. Their voices, I soon knew, at once trapped within and the very air which filled the bubble where they'd bowed out.

—The sacrifices we've made. One of us should tell them how it really is.

—Nothing special here, but I've been able to keep my wife comfortable at home.

—Cheers!

—My last kid is about to graduate junior college. All paid for.

—Huzzah!

—Little Jenny just took a job. It only took her three months post graduation—I couldn't be prouder.

—How are the benefits?

—Top-notch.

—Bravo!

—You wanna know what makes this country tick? Honor, respect, men like us.

—And a barrel of Old Style.

—Bottoms up, boys.

—We did what had to be done as fathers in the face of the American night.

—That's a decent line, Barry. Bring that novel out and write that one down.

—I look in that mirror, my friends, and and see a fucking library of novels. Men like us, we live it.

The faces drank, heads nodding, as the routines were met with the approval and one-upmanship of the crowd. Each beer pinching their pasture back a little further, as I would try my hardest to fall into the looking-glass, eager for something else other than oblivious, obnoxious fatherhood.

CHAPTER TWO

One drunken night I grew sullen, impatient, and I climbed over the bar to touch the mirror. I put my finger on the glass but it did not meet the tip of the finger in the reflection—there was a gap between them which transfixed me. As I began to push harder, intent on the two rejoining, a memory raced across my mind of a night in my early 20s.

Soon after moving to Chicago I began hearing about a writer who had once lived in my neighborhood, composing novels about the streets and people long before I arrived. He would drink in the bars up and down Division Street. I had answered an ad in *The Chicago Reader* calling for writers to pitch ideas for a new community newspaper, and the editor told me to meet her at one of those bars, The Gold Star. She offered me the position, unpaid and undefined, but I would write about the city and they would publish it. She left and I stayed behind, drinking and staring at the mirror behind the bar, romanticizing the sparkle of the silver blemishes and bubbles. I knew all I needed to do was look, watch, be and write. The rest would take care of itself.

Lost in this memory, not realizing my fingertip had begun to bruise, I saw the wings of my guardian angel unfurl in the reflection. I felt my cowering spirit burst forth from the inner chamber where it had been hiding. A strength flooded my entire body. A beautiful and overwhelming feeling of myself. I tried to extend my arms and dive in but I could not budge. The regulars began to shout and I felt two arms sliding under my own. Jeremiah had me in a full nelson and began to drag me away.

That cold October night I walked home from The Anvil absolutely loaded. Living in the far north of the city above where Lake Shore Drive ends, the east-west streets of my neighborhood ran directly into the shore. At the end of every block I was met by a giant gust of arctic Lake Michigan wind. On Thorndale, I stopped in front of the decrepit storefronts and realized the feeling had vanished, my spirit had receded. I cursed the seasons and I chided myself for believing in the barroom mirror.

The girders of the L rattled as an approaching train roared overhead. I watched the lit faces behind the train car windows, their lost eyes and magical city aura. Didn't they know all was once possible. All was once left at our front stoops in the night, if only we'd get out of bed and open our doors to receive it.

CHAPTER THREE

For quite a while after, I did not go out. I stayed home with Michelle and our kids. We'd walk up to a playground and follow the kids around making sure they did not fall off. Or we'd go to Lickity-Split for ice cream. I began reading *The Lord of the Rings* to them every night. The weight of the ring on Frodo Baggins, the urgency of the task at hand, the many decent and magical beings endangered by absolute power. Maybe there was something in here that could teach them to bear the weight better than I.

Laid-off in my mid-30s with kids, I had recently realized that nothing I set out to accomplish in my 20s as a writer had been realized. I felt snowed in, ready to abandon my dreams for a job, but terrified by the prospect of living life half-mast. How easy Sauron can creep in when the flame has been allowed to ember too long.

—How do you two like it so far?

—Daddy, Miller fell asleep.

—What about you, Penny?

—I love it!

—Are the trolls funny or scary?

—I don't get scared, Daddy.

—Woof! Woof!

—Daddy! Don't do that!

—Sorry, Penny. Come here, Daddy's a nice doggy.

—You didn't scare me.

—What do you think about this ring Frodo must carry?

—Rings are adventures.

—I love that—you're so smart. Want to hear what I have been thinking about while reading it?

—I'm tired, Daddy.

—Somehow, somewhere a ring is given to us, Penny. Many rings, and we must sort through them and recognize which one to carry for the greater good and which ones weigh us down and destroy our golden souls.

—Dadda Momma ring.

—Miller you sly dog—you were awake.

—Ruff! Ruff!

—Woof!

—I thought your dad was going to be a bit more heavy-handed than that.

—Mama, are your rings adventures?

—Your father didn't propose to me with a ring. He despises this faux wealth and security which rules us all. He wants to cast the power that corporate culture bestows on us into the fiery pits from which they were created.

—Mama, don't spoil the ending!

—That's why your mom spends her days working downtown and your dad has so much time to read you thousand-page books, keeping you up past bedtime.

—But kids, your mom used to spend her nights with your dad in Wicker Park lofts, reading long books and figuring out how we would position ourselves economically and philosophically against the notion of prized material wealth.

—Then there was that winter I had to toss the books into the fire just to stay warm. Are you putting my angels to bed or are you going out tonight, Satchel?

Soon enough I returned to The Anvil and the regulars asked where I had been. A few beers in, one of them handed me a book he said might be the best book by any Chicago author. Still staring in the mirror, I watched *One L* slide from the other end of the bar as it skimmed through the beer puddles and knocked a fresh pint into my lap. They chuckled.

—Read it and don't worry about your wet pants, young man. One day you'll understand.

Jeremiah threw me a towel and I wiped myself off. Then I picked up the book.

—Scott Turow? He's not a fucking writer.

—You're out of your mind. Read that book and thank me later by buying a few rounds when you get your first paycheck as an attorney.

—I should've studied law.

—Nah. No judge would've ever been sympathetic to a face like yours.

Had I been wrong about so much? Humbled, I read a blurb on the back of the mass market paperback copy with gray pages now bulging with beer. *A wonderful book. It should be read by anyone who has ever contemplated going to law school. Or anyone who has ever worried about being human.*

—One idiotic blurb like this diminishes the accomplishments of a century of poets and philosophers.

—You have two kids, a wife, and you think literature will feed them? Will a literary work keep your wife at your side? Listen to our friend down there. He has your best interest in mind.

—When your wife leaves you for some businessman, that fucking hurts.

—I think Turow was buddy-buddy with Wannstedt. Back in the day.

—What else do you need to know—the guy is legit.

I turned back to the mirror, said fuck it, and I began to read.

Chapter Four

I finished *One L* in a week, hypnotized by the vision of myself running with the alphas at Harvard, clamoring for the top.

That winter I applied to law schools. But my plan to become a lawyer was interrupted.

It was the Wednesday night after Christmas. We were staying at Michelle's parents' house for the holidays, and in a dream, I saw a horse running across a race track with other horses at his heels. He dug in to fight them off and pulled away to win the race. Somehow I knew the horse's name was San Giacomo.

I woke up from this dream, wrote it down and wondered if I had just peered into the future. I searched the *Daily Racing Form* and I found him, entered in a race that Friday at Hawthorne. I spent hours and hours parsing out the sick reality of believing such a thing, the beautiful magic if it were to be true.

As my law school application floated across the admissions desks, I gathered up the dollars in my wallet, in Michelle's wallet, and I brought my jar of coins to Jewel's and paid the 9% fee to cash in, dumping them into the machine by the candy dispensers, wondering how much was there. $37. Giving me $117 to bet on my dream horse.

There were no OTBs on the northside near where we lived, so I took the Red Line to North and Clybourn, and walked the rest of the way to the Mud Bug. The crowd was one of my favorite spectacles in the city. Initially I'd find a table relatively distant from the conversationalists, but as the years went by and I came in more and more, even began to feel I knew a thing or two, I'd sit anywhere the same as I would in a cafe, open to the small talk and reveling in the potential camaraderie, which honestly never materialized.

On the day I went to bet San Giacomo, I walked in, paid the two dollars entrance and bought the *Daily Racing Form*. Early and eager, I drifted through the rooms, looking for a horse's name to jump off the screen of one of the many tvs overhead, compelling me to bet it, and I took in the regulars, knowing none of their names.

In the back was the only other guy near my age. He had gray streaks in his hair and funky glasses and in my mind was a real addict, distant and talking to no one. I felt a tension between us, and we never spoke.

The trinkets guy was setting up shop, unpacking all his lucky charms from his backpack, as he did everyday. Little gnomes and figurine giraffes, as well as a receptionist's bell, two plastic hands that clapped, a whizzy spinner, and other items to make a racket with whenever a horse of his came in, which wasn't too often.

There were a few talking to themselves, others talking to the race, berating the jockeys and the horses. Some regulars never sat down, going from tv to tv, race to race, never knowing more than the number of the horse they bet. They had lucky numbers, which like their name was a birthright they held onto for direction in the open seas of life and horse racing.

One was a real mess and I loved him for it. Tall, googly-eyed, a real mumbler and a loner, but his dedication could not be doubted. Like most in this room, he was all in. As I passed him he was watching the end of a race leaning back against the wall, slowly sliding down as he softly gave his dwindling root.

—Come on 4, 7. Get into it. Get up. Get up. 4, 7. Come on 4,7. Get up. Get up. Whip him. Whip whip that 4, 7. Get up.

I glanced at the race and saw the 4 was in the picture but the seven was up the track. I wondered how long one could hold out hope and when one should turn the page to the next race. But I knew myself the times when I would stare at the screen after my horse had lost, expecting a different result, a foul and a change in order maybe, up until the results were posted *official*. How quickly a horse race transforms something that the gambler feels is inevitable into the most idiotic notion ever to have coursed through the mind. It can be hard to let go.

There was a seat open next to the guy who went through the form with colored pens, but he was always too intrusive, chatting away when someone was obviously trying to get a bet in or watch a race. Instead of sitting with him, I took a stool at the bar, meaning I had to buy a beer, leaving me with $113 to bet. Luckily, San Giacomo's race was early in the card and I kept my composure, not wasting my bank roll on knee jerk whims.

San Giacomo's odds ended up at 6-5. He pulled away and won for fun, putting nine lengths between him and the field. I didn't know if I should tell anyone that I had dreamt of the winner of that race or play it cool. I was amazed. I cashed my ticket and received $124.30 on top of my initial bet, finished my beer, bundled up and headed out into the bitter cold to hop the Red Line back home. That's all I won? I was given the winner by my dreams, a sure thing, and that's all I bet? This magical strange occurrence, how unreal, and all that I got out of it was enough for one trip to the grocery store. I began to feel anxious, like some god was watching me, laughing, so I tried to empty my mind and focus on breathing deeply. More dreams would come and I simply needed to bet more next time.

Soon after, I found out I got into law school, but I could not convince myself to accept. I asked for an extension. When that expired, I asked for one more.

CHAPTER FIVE

On April 25, the day before I had to let the admissions officer know, I still had no idea what I should do.

That morning began like most during this stretch. I got my bike out of the basement and rode to Metropolis, the café a few blocks up Kenmore from our apartment. I ordered coffee and talked with the baristas; I nodded to the Northwestern Professor who took his coffee there every morning and I found a seat in the window. My writing had flown off the creative rails, stuck in the rut of introspective, self-analyzing journaling. That day's topic was the decision at hand: Law School. I played out the fork in front of me fantasizing each way and how I would change as I went along.

There was no clarity to be had, all of it bombastic and narcissistic. Reading it back over, I scared myself right out of my café seat and hopped on my bike to ride up two more blocks to Berger Park, where most days I ate my peanut butter sandwich lunch.

Overlooking the churning blue waters, though times were dire, I wondered how it could get any better than this—all alone as if no one knew this secret Chicago view, lost in the waters and the sun. The shoreline had been a part of my transformation, having moved to Edgewater from Wicker Park, where previously I lived to smoke cigarettes and brood across the streets. In Edgewater I quit smoking, brooded less and picked up jogging along Lake Shore Path. This to offset the depression, which Michelle and I lightened up a bit by calling *compression*, that Chicago conjures across the soul.

An interesting notion came to me that morning: I am what I see. Meaning that yes, how I register what I see is dependent on my thinking, but further than that, I am locatable outside of myself. I am the waters I see. I am the tree. The ornamentation on the building. The intersection of Belmont and Clark. My I is further reaching than myself.

I practiced being conscious of this as I walked along where Sheridan curves west to avoid Lake Michigan, watching the waters crash beneath Loyola University whose buildings face the sea, permanently awaiting Chicago's promise to extend the shoreline. Then one easy block over to The Coffee Shop, the liberal Jewish outpost positioned strategically across the street from the Jesuit college. I added to this philosophical turn of consciousness that the way I see the world is the way I see myself, and then I put it to bed and spent the rest of the early afternoon betting the horses.

Tammie ran the front of the house at The Coffee Shop

and Jake did constant odd jobs and maintenance around the building. He was as calm and mellow as late mid-century American psychedelic culture can make them. They took no pretenses with their cafe—the lights were bright, no music, the coffee weak and warm, not hot, kids toys in the back, the tables in disarray. It was a place where Tammie maternally got to know you. A piano in the corner and the guitar always out, a plate with condoms and dental dam at the door, a $3 egg sandwich, $5 for the brisket, and they stayed open until midnight, a rarity in Chicago unless booze was served. Tammie knew I was a teacher, Jake knew I was a writer, and for months I sat in the back by the toys with my laptop screen facing away from the customers, streaming races on TVG, placing bets, in a zone.

—Look at you, Satchel, back for more.

—What can you do?

—The *chutzpah*. After the beating you took yesterday?

—It's horse racing.

—Honestly, those photo finishes?

—My guy Pawlowski from the Mud Bug taught me to be decision-oriented.

—Hey Jake, do we know any Pawlowski? I think that's the Polish family we used to swap recipes with for meat and onion dishes.

—It's all meat and onions for those Poles, Tammie.

—Where are the kids? I told you I'll watch the kids.

—Listen, Satchel. People who know what they are doing can be decision-oriented, but throw a handful of rocks in a crowd and tell me how many people who get stoned know what they are doing. Right, Tammie?

—Jake, you've been getting stoned for years and still know your salt.

—I love this woman.

—Where's your wife in all this? Is she decision-oriented?

—Tammie, she is decision-oriented up until a point, but the dry spells put a look in her eyes that screams we need results.

—Can't blame her my *bubala*. A mother wants to hear the *tachlis*.

—Here she goes. Whenever we cook brisket, out pours the Yiddish.

—Tammie, today's the day. Egg sandwich and coffee.

—Dark or light roast?

—Whichever one's fresh, hot, and not weak.

—Not weak? As in strong? Should send this guy to school across the street, Jake.

—He's a writer, Tammie, let him word away.

—You know Jake took some classes down at Columbia.

—I was working on a screenplay.

—You two with your words. We don't have cheddar. How's muenster?

—I like swiss.

—You can poke holes in swiss.

—There's a lot I like that you can poke holes in. What was the film?

—It's called *Silver and Gold*.

—Give him the pitch, Jake—maybe he can help you out.

—Alright. A talk-of-the-town metalsmith discovers a cave full of gold when on a retreat in Israel. He brings it back to Chicago, right, and begins making gold jewelry. Beautiful pieces but odd enough that his old customers do not appreciate the artistry. Nor can they afford their price tag. He has to attract wealthier clients, people he doesn't know and are not part of his *mishpachah*. Now you got me doing it, Tammie. His reputation goes *flush* and though his jewelry sells at top dollar, he loses his friends, his wife, and in the middle of a bender to end all benders, he has a vision.

—Before we became so sanitized and civilized, Satchel, visions and the voice of God were a part of everyday life. Abraham, Jesus, Muhammad—these holy men were all just one of many.

—Yes, but they had the conviction to act on what they heard. And undoubtedly they were charismatic, you can't just write those spiritual leaders off.

—Jake, I wasn't. Just getting the facts straight.

—In his vision, he sees a modest iron-smelting cauldron being filled with anything and everything: metal, plant, cloud, cloth, animal, and he watched it begin to pour into new molds. Shapes he'd never seen before, marvelous wonders before his eyes, some gigantic, some itsy-bitsy, all of them impossible to wear. This wasn't jewelry—this was art. He realized the material didn't matter, it was the vision which he must illuminate. The next day he quit and began his life as an artist tending to this vision. As he is leaving Chicago, he is kidnapped by the Mossad.

—Jake, your symbolism is lost on this *goy*. Silver represents the righteous ones. Those who funnel the divine into the everyday world. Gold represents those who once struggled with darkness but have emerged on a path towards transcendence.

—After a grueling interrogation, quite a few killer near-death chase scenes, and sexy trysts with these beautiful and rich jewelry-loving women, the metalsmith escapes the Mossad, he meets a woman who lives in the streets and she captures his heart. Perfection, beauty—he is transfixed by the joy she resonates, and he realizes she is God's greatest creation.

—In my opinion, here's where the story goes *kaput*.

—And he has a hippy epiphany. There is no need for humans to make new forms. This is the work of God. He didn't fully comprehend his initial vision—he was witnessing the core cauldron of God, not of man. His vision was of the generative core of God's creative energy. So he joins this mysterious and lovely woman and they begin to wander the earth intent on appreciating all that is in the name of God.

—That's how it ends?

—*Schmutz*, all *schmutz*.

—I was never good with endings.

—Well you got a great plot.

—The chase scenes, Satchel. I could've been the next John Woo.

—The heavy themes are great for conversation in the cafe, but once you step out these doors, people want the *tachlis*.

—She means the brass tacks, Satchel.

—Who's John Woo?

—*Mission Impossible 2*, baby.

—That reminds me. There's a horse in the 5th at Aqueduct named Brass Tacks.

—You're gonna bet him?

—Don't steal all the Wi-Fi. Those horse races jam up the broadband. The kids will be over to study any minute.

—Today's the day, Tammie.

—Keep at it, Satchel—there's a twinkle in your eyes and the vision could be just around the corner for you.

—Don't I want the gold?

—Jake, he didn't hear a word you said.

—Everyone wants the silver, the gold. But if you can see the world for what it is, you'll realize you already possess anything you might want from such materials.

—Your coffee is up. I'll bring your breakfast over.

I walked across the linoleum floors, beneath the fluorescent lights, and found a seat at my favorite table mod-podged with American folk recipes for common household items. I opened my computer and pulled out my horse notebook.

I had woken up that morning remembering my dream. It was all based on my Irish, horse-owning friends Cap and Sonny. They were getting drunk. And moving through a house party. There was music playing, and they were arguing, and the song playing was "Love Shack" by the B-52s. Then the room got dark and they walked down a corridor, sliding back a curtain to reveal a Metallica album, *Master of Puppets*.

It felt revelatory. When I awoke, I immediately swung my legs out of bed, grabbed for my laptop and glasses, and scanned the entries on the Irish tracks. Outside of Dublin at Leopardstown they were running a night card, and in the 2nd race there was a horse named B-52. There was also a horse named Master of Puppets. I swelled with the confusion of the magic. I did not follow the Irish horses. I did not listen to these bands.

Tammie brought my sandwich.

—You should really bring your kids. I'll watch them. That one, she is a cutie.

—Penny.

—She's something.

—There's a horse in the 5th named Penny. Think I should bet it Tammie?

—Don't bet your kids, Satchel. He's betting his kids' names, Jake!

—He's an old-timer. That's what my dad did.

—His dad died broke. Don't bet your kids, Satchel.

It was a 5-furlong turf sprint. B-52 was at 34-1. Master of Puppets 12-1. You never know how a trifecta will pay out but with the win bet, exacta bet, and trifecta, I stood to win $60,000 if B-52 won and Master of Puppets finished second. $18,000 if at least one of the two dream horses came in 1st. I'd come a long way from just dreaming of a

31

6-5 shot.

At Leopardstown, 5 furlongs was a straight dash, no turns. Eighteen horses broke from the gate and began shredding the grass with their hoofs, churning muscle, nostril-flaring havoc, these 1000-pound beasts slamming into one another, jockeys waving their crops, snarling for the finish line. B-52 broke a step slow but Master of Puppets got out clean. Already saturated with adrenaline, a late surge from B-52 squeezed my heart through my eyes. Photo finish.

They take forever with these photo finishes. But when the stewards made their ruling and they put the results on the screen, B-52 came up in 2nd. Master of Puppets in 3rd. All my kill bets went through one of them winning.

But I had bet B-52 to place, *either way* is what they call it in Ireland, and that paid enough to cover the costs of the bets. Zero sum but teetering on the edge of a life-changing score—a horse length away.

—Looks like I am going to law school, Tammie.

—You hit one?!

—No. Just missed. All these just-misses makes me think I ought to veer left.

—We've been veering left since the sixties, kid.

—I thought a big score would pay for your schooling, Satchel.

—I got a scholarship, all good there.

—At Loyola here?

—Loyola in New Orleans.

—Well you didn't tell us you were of that persuasion.

—Attorney?

—Pagan.

—Yeah, last thing the world needs is another pagan lawyer.

—You two are the best.

—Don't go far from us Satchel, we'll keep you honest.

I walked out of there zero sum. This was before I knew the truth that very few if any longtime professional horseplayers could survive without getting rebates: 10-15% of every dollar they bet paid back to them from the corporate bookies they bet with. Which made it all about heavy churn, pushing money through the windows, trying to break even, and living off that 10-15%. To break even was success.

Chapter Six

I unlocked my bike and tooled around a little looking to see who was out, what was what. Lakeside of Broadway consisted of three north-south streets. Winthrop and Kenmore were lined with ornate, handsome apartment buildings from the 1880s, simple 6-flat numbers with a decorative cornice and brick sunrooms that jutted out. Any raised in the building boom of the 1940s were replaced by four-plus-ones which were 5-story brick rectangles covering three or four lots with parking on the bottom. Sheridan was lined with high-rise cement and glass apartment buildings overlooking the lake beaches to the east and Chicago's residential grid to the west.

The Red Line stopped at three east-west streets: Granville, Thorndale and Bryn Mawr, making these the commercial strips. Derelict, hard-nosed people were running errands, grabbing a meal, on their way to the trains to head to work, hitting up the diner for a reasonably-priced cup of coffee, stopping by the podiatry storefront for cushioned sole shoes.

I biked down Granville past The Anvil where the door was open and three people were laughing at something the bartender said. I considered going in but the afternoon crowd was always a few rungs below where I wanted to go.

I crossed to the other side of the street so I could continue peering inside inconspicuously, wondering about these bar flies while leaning against my bike and chewing nicorette. Lost in disparaging thoughts—I was a real bully thinker for some time—I came to when a man and two kids waved goodbye to the bartender and emerged from the shadows past the drinkers in the door, stepping out onto the street. I had this guy in my sights. What a fucking loser—take your kids to a bar with hope at least.

Then they shouted at me.

—Hey! Daddy!

—Dadda!

It was Penny and Miller. The man with them was Dennis, their daytime babysitter.

—What are you doing here?

They crossed the street.

—Don't run Miller.

Miller started to cry thinking I yelled at him and was angry. I leaned down and gave him a hug and he hit me in the chest.

—Mean Dadda!

Dennis was right behind them.

—Well, there's your dad, kids. Hi, Satchel.

—What's going on? Why were you all at the bar?

—Looking for you, Daddy.

—I'll be home in a little bit, Penny. You don't need to worry.

—Satchel, sorry to be short but I have to run. Michelle said you would be home by 2:30 at the latest.

—What time is it?

—3:30.

—Oh fuck.

Dennis covered Penny's ears.

—Pay me next time. It's fine. I'm supposed to be reffing at the Windy City Rollers.

—Dennis, I'm sorry, man. I can't believe I forgot. Who's playing tonight?

—Helles Belles versus the Double Crossers.

—Badass.

Penny covered Miller's ears.

—Sorry to scare you there, I wasn't sure where to find you and the kids mentioned this bar. Bye kids!

—Bye Denny!

—Bye bye.

Chapter Seven

By 5:30 pm I had begun cooking dinner in the middle of the dirty dishes and littered countertop, cursing Nicorette gum and trying to convince myself to smoke in front of the kids. We ate almost every meal together as a family, and our kids had grown to love it. The attention, the talk, the laughing and goofing off, the food. Parenting is a strange game, so little of the positive stuff comes from what you say, so much of it from what you do. You can fuck your kid up by your choice of words. Parenting is one of the only situations out there where you get worse as you go along. You are the best you will ever be at the beginning, when you have not been dragged through the child's gauntlet of tantrums, crying and negotiating, all the fears and worries. When you hold your baby that first day after being born, pure love, all affection and tender care, that is the best parent you will ever be. It's all a dumbshow after that, and it gets dumber every year. Many say that the teenage years are the worst, teenagers are so difficult, but really, it's that parents have gotten to their lowest and worst level, never able to say the right thing, never able to make the right decision, provide the proper amount and quality of love. If you could hold your teenager with as much pure affection as you did that newborn, those years would be fine. If you could stop filling their heads with unsolicited advice and disparaging remarks.

Michelle broke the silence.

—Did you apply to that blog?

—The one here in town?

—Is there another one?

—Which one are you thinking of?

—Have you applied anywhere?

—I told you about Latin and Parker, right?

—Besides the high school teaching jobs that won't start for another year.

—Not yet.

And then silence.

—Do you think I should?

—I don't know.

—Well, why did you want to know then?

—No reason.

—Dennis said the kids took good naps. Three hours for Miller, just over two for Penny.

—Don't call him Miller. Hank, eat your peas.

—Miller wasn't named after Henry Aaron. He did eat them, when you weren't looking.

—What else is happening when I'm not looking?

—What's your deal?

—What did you do while we were paying Dennis to

watch them take naps?

At that time I was never proud of what I did with my days because it never produced the answer which put me at the helm to right our ship.

—You know I'm writing. The house is clean, right? Dinner, it's cooked.

—Satchel, just find a job. The stress is getting to me.

—Unemployment pays me as much as you earn—we're fine.

—When will those checks end?

—Obama keeps extending it. Kids, cheers to Uncle Obama.

—Cheers!

—I've got to make the law school decision tomorrow.

—What'd you decide?

—Tonight. Let's drink a bottle of wine, maybe with Koan if she's out back, and finally figure it out. —Koan told me Bodhi's still traveling. I saw her on my way in.

—Is Bodhi still gone? That's actually better—I don't want to hear what he has to say.

—How about tomorrow night we have a bottle of wine down by the beach? The kids can play—I'll get some food together, a little picnic.

—Sounds good but what about tonight?

—We've got company tonight. My high school friends.

Didn't we talk about this?

—No. Like Margo and Emily?

—Like the whole group.

—Who?

—Those two and their husbands. Kristen. Laura. And like Steve, Kyle, Chris. Fred.

—What the fuck?

—Satchel, cool it.

—Those pieces of shit aren't welcome here.

—Of course they are.

—I'm not sitting around listening to those people. Definitely not tonight.

—We're just getting together to celebrate. Chris and Fred sold their business.

—I've heard all about it. From you, your parents—a fucking million times.

—It's one night. They're bringing champagne and a spread from Greek Town.

—No. Cancel it.

—I won't. They've also got a new project—something maybe that's up your alley. You can hear them out. It'll be fine.

—You can't tell me about how they all used to try and break us up, then expect me to hang out with them, let alone have them over and discuss what? Working for

40

them?

—We've gone over this so many times—that's not what I meant. I should have never said anything.

—You didn't need to say anything for me to know what they think about me. Fuck guys like that.

—I don't go out every week like you. I need to see people. They're just being sweet to come over so I don't have to pay for a babysitter.

—See people, do that, I agree, but go see your friends, have your friends over. Those guys are not friends.

—Who are my other friends? Gershwin? Nightingale and Dunbar? I work and have two kids, no friends.

—I agree, you've seemed lonely, Michelle. it sucks.

—I know they suck. But everybody has been missing each other ever since losing Nathan.

—You don't think they're coming over to rag on me?

—It's not about you, Satch.

—They tried to break us up. They've filled your head with insults about me since day one.

—It didn't work, Satchel. Get over it—we are married, have kids—so who cares what they said or didn't say.

—Whatever. I don't want them in my head right now—they are the last thing I need.

—Maybe they know people who can help you find work.

—Of course. I'm going out.

—I thought you quit The Anvil.

—You're right. I'll go to LeSabre.

—Be a deadbeat, fine, but don't act surprised when they call you a deadbeat.

—There you go.

—I did not invite them. They insisted.

—Although you never said no to Fred while we were dating, you could have said no now.

She slapped me and Penny began to cry. Miller messed the food around his high chair, knocking beans and carrots all over the wall and rug.

—Bye.

I downplayed the slap, giving it a quick rub with the back of my hand and tasting for blood, then I leaned in and kissed each kid.

—Looks like mommy and daddy are fighting with each other like Penny and Miller sometimes do. That wasn't nice, was it?

—Dadda? Mama hit Dadda?

—She should say sorry, right Miller?

—Sorry Dadda?

Finally processing it, or sad because she was unable to process it, Penny began to cry.

—Dad's not mad, Penny. Mom just made a mistake.

42

She had a tough day at work. You two be good, but don't be too nice to those mean men who are coming over to Dad's house tonight, alright?

—Okay, Dadda.

—Jesus, you never quit.

I stood up and went to get my keys, wallet, and messenger shoulder bag. I took my computer out, and I grabbed a couple beers from the fridge, the joint I kept rolled for when I needed a joint, situated it all along with *One L,* which I couldn't stop rereading. Michelle stopped me in the kitchen on my way out.

—I'm sorry, Satchel. I shouldn't have done that. I know you've been there to listen to me talk about it all but Nathan dying has been hard to process. I haven't seen these friends except at the funeral, and I want to see them, okay? Okay?

—Okay. I get it—that makes sense. But I'm not sticking around.

—They're just looking out for me. I'll text you.

—Any clarity I had is gone.

—Your precious decision making—it's too much.

CHAPTER EIGHT

I hadn't planned on going out. The Anvil was out of the question, I knew what they would say, so I texted Gershwin, an old student of mine, to see if he would be at LeSabre.

—*Yo! You hitting up the Riv tonight?*

—*Satchmo you old-timer no need to text I'll be there*

—*Heading down now but you know the long haul.*

—*C ya when i c ya just have to swing by Coup de Brew at some point*

—*You going to blow it up?*

—*Lol, might be working there. More later.*

—*No Thrill Jockey?*

A while back, Gershwin had taken a job as a producer with a local record label to work with musicians in the studio. It had been a few years since he put out an album himself, and I could see his wheels spinning, so I encouraged him to take the job at the time, thinking it might shake the rust off. Thrill Jockey put out albums very similar to Gershwin's first album, and he was doing good work bringing in bands and putting his unique spin on their songs. My last text hung out there, so It looked like I'd have to wait to find out more.

At LeSabre were the people I wanted to know, but it

was twelve miles away and the crowd was a good five to ten years younger. I felt distant. To get there on the CTA, I would take the Red Line to the Pink and then walk down Halsted, or the Broadway bus to the Halsted bus, spanning 78 blocks through the slowest moving driving in the city. Or I would ride my bike, which is what I mostly did, taking the lake path and then cutting from Soldier Field to Cermak through the South Loop. Immersed in the sea of buildings and crowded intersections, conversations and style of random Chicagoans, the glimmering lake waters and canopy of trees, the expressways, lit windows, storefront restaurants, the smells and night skies—my bike rides shaped my thinking during that time. When we lived in Wicker Park, I walked everywhere, but up in Edgewater, there was too much ground to cover.

We lived on the third floor and our neighbors' apartment shared a wall with ours, but there was nothing separating our back deck, which faced east towards the lake. They spent as much time out there as we did. The Magus family, like it or not, were in our lives, listening, reflecting, likely judging after overhearing our fights.

I shut the back door from the kitchen. Koan and her daughter Maya sat across from each other on the broken seats I helped Bodhi drag up from the alley earlier in the winter, which he mended one evening using palm caning

45

he had found years prior and had been saving in the basement.

A junior in high school, Maya sat below the Tibetan prayer flags that hung along the roof line. She leaned in bringing a needle and thread into another patch she was adding to her denim jacket. Koan, a harmonium player who taught music at the Lycée Français, sat with her legs folded as she stitched up a pair of ripped jeans, her head of wild hair at the center of the threadbare mandala tapestry that hung across the painted brick wall, a glass of wine at her side. Her husband Bodhi was a rabbit-out-of-a-hat magician who left for long stretches as he traveled to drum up shows, busking on streets in cities around the world. Or so he told us but you never know.

—*Ciao!*

—Is Bodhi back tonight?

—Yes. We believe so.

—Good. I was worried he had vanished.

Maya looked up, squinting playfully at me.

I took a few steps towards her to perform my ritual. Everytime I left out the back I would rub the prayer flag between my fingers. The wind horse. Faded from the sun rays that filtered through the elm and catalpa trees and dappled our deck each morning, I took solace in the many years the prayer flags had hung there, the many breezes blown through them.

—The good fortune of the wind horse comes from letting go, not holding on.

—You've noticed. I love that one.

—Has it brought you luck with the ponies?

—That's what it is? Luck?

—No, I guess there is more to it. Maya and I were just speaking about it the other day.

—I found a wind horse patch, see? I love it, the way it reminds me that the energy I need is always there.

—As long as the winds keep blowing.

—Your senior year starts soon.

—Would you mind reading over my college essays?

—Alright but I've been a little sentimental recently so if you hear me saying more emotion, more depth, just slap me.

—Going out alone tonight? Maybe we'll invite Michelle over for wine.

—She has friends coming over but I bet they end up joining you out here. LeSabre is calling my name.

—Maya, where is Bodhi's regular spot?

—Where he drinks that Malört stuff?

—Yes, it's much closer. The company there are artists like you, yes?

—Oh, Simon's?

—That's the one.

—Opposite of the wind horse you might say.

—You don't think it's just too much Malört?

—I do drink too much, no shaking that.

—We know. We hear you yelling.

They looked at each other and grinned.

—That's Wolfgang downstairs, not me.

—He's that loud?

—He's just fed up with Obama, hates him.

—He is … how do you say it, Maya? A caveman.

—I yell at my kids plenty but I know Uncle Obama has my back.

—The Tribune just ran an article saying they won't extend the unemployment benefits. It's been 99 weeks since the entire recession.

—You're kidding me?

—Positive news about the economy, no?

—Maya, stay in school. It's a nightmare out here.

—A nightmare with a few nice bars.

Again their grin.

—I better go before the kids start crying at Michelle and I get puffed up with heroic guilt.

—Michelle seemed sad when I told her about the end of the benefits—we talked when she came home from work.

—Michelle hates Obama.

—No!?

—Ask her over wine. Those jeans you two are sewing look kickass. *Tre chíc.*

—My mom is always at the center of fashion.

—Look to the heavens tonight—a full moon.

—Maybe I'll see it rising over the lake.

And I headed down the stairs.

—Have fun on your wind horse.

I didn't need to look back to see them smiling at that one.

CHAPTER NINE

I considered picking up the mess of crayons and figurines which had dropped onto Wolfgang's deck, but decided not to when I saw the curtain rustling from behind the glass door. I didn't need another delay, though I could hear Alice had company on her deck below.

A detective for the Chicago Police Department, Alice despised me. On the other hand, she had a crush on Michelle, and she would switch from a flat-faced annoyance when talking with me to a bright-eyed engagement as Michelle talked about anything, it didn't matter, what she bought at the farmer's market or the upcoming closure of the Thorndale stop.

Her softball team gathered around the patio table drinking Budweiser and eating handfuls of Vitners chips. They all had black streaks under their eyes, and Alice had pushed her Oakley shades atop her dirty blonde hair pulled tight into a ponytail. Their team was sponsored by The Anvil and a few were still in uniform. A few in their sponsored undershirts. Their mascot was a woman police officer firing a gun with an anvil discharging instead of a bullet. They were called The Anvil Arsenal.

—Bright out there? Who'd you all play?

—What did that guy say?

—He lives upstairs.

—Oh, must be *that* guy.

—We lost to the Hollywood Hammocks.

—Thanks for asking, Satchel. Good night.

—What kind of name is Satchel?

—Dope-smokers' name is what it is.

—I heard something about a new dog.

—Fuck this guy. Pass the sour cream..

Her last rescue dog bit Miller, as well as Koan, and I had knocked on her door and told her it had to go. I guess her girlfriend at that time loved that dog more than she loved Alice because she left, too, and Alice blamed me for ruining her relationship.

—Looks like a pit bull.

—It's a boxer.

—Is it? Seems like one angry boxer.

—You're one to talk.

—Keep it inside.

—It's a boxer. But I'll tell you what. You can check its papers if I can check your pockets.

—Tell him what's up, Alice.

—I know you'd rather check Michelle's pockets.

—Motherfucker.

And she stood up, puffed out, and got in my face. A cop is a cop is a cop.

—Listen, I'm off duty when I'm home. But you are endangering your children. I've had a few long talks with Dennis. I know the fucking score.

—The score is Hammocks one, Anvils zero.

In a breathtaking instant she grabbed my wrist, spun me around and pulled my arm up behind my back.

—Nobody fucks with The Anvil Arsenal.

—Nobody!

—Maybe you didn't hear me, Satchel. Or should I call you Scrotum?

—That's goddamn hilarious, Alice!

—DCFS. I'll call. I will. Those kids need a dad, not a faggot artist.

—Let go.

—Or what?

She tightened her grip and then dropped my arm and pushed me back.

—Take care of your wife, too. Or I'll take care of her for you.

I walked down the last steps rubbing my wrist, wondering if I should yell at her or not. My mind raced for something cutting, something brutal, some combination of words that would hurt not only her but all the CPD, and all of Chicago for that matter. A breeze came through and I heard the faint laughter of Koan and Maya on the third floor. Hurting people is no fun.

I unlocked the basement door, grabbed my bike and wheeled past the laundry machines and our recycling bins, looking around to make sure I was alone. Last week one morning I had come down to grab my bike, and there was a man sitting on the washer I had never seen before: ragged clothes, an unkempt beard, and a yeasty stench. When he slid off the machine and stepped toward me, mumbling, I noticed he was a good six inches taller than I and had his hands in his pockets feeling around, searching. He kicked at an overstuffed cloth bag, filled with his possessions, and a plaid shirt spurted out.

—I need a *lawyer.*

—What? This ain't a law firm, man.

—I need two *lawyers.*

I struggled to understand him, like he had a swollen tongue. I leaned in and squinted my eyes. For some reason I do that when trying to hear.

—What are you doing here?

—*Lawyer.*

—Who are you staying with?

—Two would be *nice.*

Lawyer. He had to be saying lawyer. Did this man appear from nowhere to tell me to be a lawyer? The encounter set me spinning and I had to walk out of there.

I tried to focus on my breath as I had learned years ago when struggling with bouts of sleep paralysis. Was I hallucinating? Was this a vision? The anxiety overtook me and I spent the day walking, lying in grass medians and on benches when the out of body experience blossomed into vertigo. Michelle was at work, so we were paying Dennis $12 an hour for me to take one more step towards a crazed life on the streets.

When I told Michelle about it she sobered me up.

—I saw him, too. But I told him to get the fuck out of our basement.

—You saw him?

—How did you let him stay there while our kids were home. He just broke in to do laundry.

—Laundry?

—He didn't say lawyer, Satchel. He was asking for a quarter.

—No.

—Yes. He asked me too, mumbling and spitting.

I sat down.

—I was about to tell you I decided on law school.

—Because some derelict mumbled *lawyer* to you?

—I thought he was a vision. And he was in our building. It seemed like it was a sign.

—You and your signs.

—That explains why Lawyer Dave didn't win today.

—You bet a horse named lawyer because of this?

—No. I didn't bet, I was too frazzled. I just had to walk around, but I almost did. I checked the race a few minutes ago, lost by a football field.

— I don't think there are forces on the other side trying to influence whether or not any of us goes to law school.

—Visions create a confusing headspace.

—I understand why you bet the horses who you dream will win. It's crazy but I get it. Don't bet the random words you see and hear during the day, okay?

—Okay.

—Listen to your dreams.

And I didn't ask her to clarify, feeling so vulnerable in my insanity, but it was the only thing I wanted to hear her say.

I wheeled my bike up the cement steps and over to the back gate by the garage. Alice and her friends were having another good laugh and tossing around high fives. I put my kickstand down and walked back so they could see me. I held my hand like a phone and put it to my ear, making sure they could hear.

—Hello, yes 911? I'd like to file a complaint on one, Alice B. Toklas. On Winthrop. Yes, that's the one. I know officer, she is one of your own. You saw this coming?

Okay. See you in 15 minutes and I do appreciate your prompt response. What's that? She used her nightstick on all the female recruits at the Academy?

She shot down her steps and almost got to me, but I hightailed it through the gate and sped down the alley, grinning and giggling like I did making prank phone calls as a kid.

—You left the backgate open, you asshole! Your wife and kids are upstairs—give me a break! DCFS!

I lifted my head and gave out a loud hoot, speeding over the speed humps on Ardmore and catching the smallest jumps. Every time I mustered the velocity to escape into the night, I realized how energized and magical the world is. The spring lake breeze bringing warm air up from the south opened up across my skin, and I smiled at the 125-year-old redstone Episcopal Church. I stopped at Sheridan, took a look behind me to make sure The Anvils weren't following me, and crossed when the traffic was clear.

Chapter Ten

Ardmore ends at the beach exactly where Lake Shore Path begins. The slow spring sunset elicited a mesmerizing glow across the lake waters, choppy with the winds and rolling along like quicksilver. Mercury. Living silver, I remembered from my Cosmology for Poets course in college, an evocative phrase. Living metal. We search for creatures like us, but the universe is full of living metal. Waves of information, intelligence. Ghost particle neutrinos. Liquid diamonds at the core of Neptune. An antimatter fountain at the center of the Milky Way where the twin gamma-ray bubbles balloon in a symmetrical spectacle of paralyzing mysteries. And here the lake water waves rise silver, fall indigo. Quicksilver Messenger Service, their 1969 psychedelic blues rock album *Happy Trails* made me feel like midnight was mine when I was a teenager, and I listened to it as I'd drive from friend's house to friend's house picking up whoever was able to go out that night. The T-1000 from *Terminator 2: Judgment Day*, an indestructible malevolent, shapeshifting mercury substance from the future sent back to kill the child John Connor. Two Terminators pitted against each other. Reprogrammed by The Resistance, the T-800 was sent back to protect the young Connor from the T-1000.

What an ending to that film. Finally Sarah Connor is shotgunning that mercurial sonofabitch to the edge of the catwalk in a foundry, almost tipping him into a vat of molten steel but she is one shell short. Then here comes T-800 rolling up on a conveyor with a grenade launcher which he pelts in T-1000's heart, exploding him into a monstrous Daliesque shape that topples into the liquid fire. We watch him in the throes of annihilation transforming back into all the people he had killed to steal their forms before finally turning completely inside out and disintegrating. T-800 then steps onto the crane as Sarah Connor drops him down, giving a final thumbs up from the Terminator.

Maybe my future law firm would send my lawyer self back to strangle my young rock n roll sorcerer self before I could ever know the thrills of a soulful expressive life which kept me from getting into attorney-hood at a sensible age.

Passing the far edge of Hollywood Beach to my left, a few people enjoying the night sky on the cement pier-steps. I could hear the inarticulable distortion of their voices across the water, a football caught in a teenager's hands, the choppy waves against the pier. The seagulls. I pedaled into the brilliant darkening night, winding through the canopy of trees imagining trolls, elves, and orcs hidden deep within all I could not see.

Zipping by the beaches, the basketball court, the magic tree grove, Montrose Harbor, the soccer fields where men from other countries played under the lights, the native grasses, the golf course, the clock tower. The Bike Shack, where I had bought this bike a year before. Belmont Harbor and my turn-off under Zoo Tunnel into Lincoln Park, the driving range and playgrounds, the Italian restaurant in the park. A cinematic rush. Joggers, bikes, strollers, teenagers, 20-somethings, elderly. All that the city hides, all that the city protects.

I felt my thigh vibrate. Probably Michelle, I thought, maybe one last point about how I should have stayed. Surely she was embarrassed by me. I didn't check.

Cutting over from the lake path just south of the Lincoln Park Zoo there is a promenade that climbs right above a pond. It overlooks a park expanding out to a wall of trees. Above and beyond, the grandeur of a layered city. First the low-rise Victorian Italianate of the late 1800s preserved by the wealth of Lincoln Park. Then Old Town which gives way to the mid-rises, the red-lettered neon Lincoln Hotel ascending through the various non-descript 80s-cement apartment towers scattered beneath the turn of the century glass-skin high-rises of the Gold Coast. As the city bends, jutting into the lake, the Drake

Hotel sits below the grand Palmolive reaching up to the pinnacle, the gray and glass Hancock climbing 100-stories tall. It is the type of view that has captured our American sensibility of what a city is—a sea of tall buildings, lit up and laced with active human mysteries. Our human approximation of a mountain range—chiseled hills showered in sparkling jewels—something you stare at and get lost with an expectation of a beautiful thought or euphoric feeling. But you never know why—it is not a logical exercise, just mesmerization.

I dropped my bike and messenger bag to the ground, cracked opened the Half Acre Over Ale tallboy, lit my joint and stood there soaking up the alcohol and marijuana to my brain, these buildings to my heart. I felt my body a site of openness. I have always wanted to be possessed by the city, to be the city, for everything that I do to be attributed to it, to Chicago. To live for it, and for it to live through me. This authenticity that sent me from Kansas City up here to begin with, twelve years ago, at the age of 22, knowing nothing but that I wanted to walk, and that I wanted to be poor, and that I wanted to live amongst non-corporate people, artists, sketchy street-corner leaning poets of place, liquor stores with guns behind the counter, prostitutes, parties in loft spaces and cigarettes, everywhere a perfect place to stop and smoke a cigarette.

As I drank, I admired my naivete, nostalgic for it. I was more open then, letting the city in, exposing myself, living at a higher rate of exposure. But with each year, I knew I had seen so much and felt like I needed to see less.

Behind me, I heard the roar of the lion echoing through the zoo. The sad truth of it all, the glory that could be, the ferocity, pure power and instinctual brutality of a wild life. I wondered what are we up to in civilization to diminish our wilderness? Creating a culture that renders bewilderment an obsolete mode of processing? We cage and we observe and we execute efficiency and maximize value, telling ourselves the story that we are making progress, never making time to tend to the social contract that all this is based upon, wincing if ever we remember we are citizens of Omelas. Still the lion roars in the heart of the city.

I was worried that I had gotten what I wished for: that I was the city, and when I looked at the city, I began to see the blemishes in an unromantic fashion. I began to notice the defects and the degeneration, and I was startled to see myself as such, to see my brain as despicable as the bricks as the lunatics as the politicians, my body as suited as Daly Square, as commercially driven as Milwaukee Avenue, corporate boardrooms defining the newest sports bar in my chest, CTA drivers methed-out at 3 a.m. plunging down my arm, my nose a dumpster and where my lion was mattered little unless I could discover an arena, an endeavor to wake up and free my wild warrior.

Climbing back on my bike, I remembered the statue of Goethe just 100 yards away, which had captured my attention often before spurring a few afternoons of research at the Harold Washington Library. It reminded me of a Greek god, how he is presented standing there bare-chested and chiseled with one foot upon an anvil and an eagle across his knee. A cape around his neck like a superhero. A whetstone in one hand and a metal sword lifted high in the other. I sought to understand why a rational and no-nonsense city like Chicago would honor an artist of such depth and profound emotion. I was not surprised to learn how poorly the sculpture was received in 1913 when erected. The committee members who commissioned the sculptor Herman Hahn stated they hoped to release Chicago artists from the trammels of costume and conventionality and permit them to give free flight to their imagination and enthusiasm. I began taking Penny and Miller to sit on the nearby bench and admire it, as they ate their popcorn just purchased at the Zoo, and read aloud to them the quote from *Faust* transcribed across its base while they fumbled to keep the popcorn from falling out of their hands on the way into their mouths.

As soon as you trust yourself, you will know how to live.
If not, you'll sit forever, gluing things together
Cooking up a stew from other's scraps
Blowing on a miserable fire
Made from your heap of dying ash.
Let apes and children praise your art
If their admiration's to your taste
But you'll never speak from heart to heart
Unless it rises up from your heart's space.

I recited these lines, which were etched into my memory, and I hoped my children's, too, as I raced through the mountain range of skyscrapers I had just beheld.

At Monroe Harbor I slowed down to admire the Michigan Avenue streetwall on my right, Michelle and I each worked in a few of these historic buildings over the years. I saw the Hilton where we spent our wedding night, waking up the orange glow of the sunrise lighting up the lake and sky. I looked into the window which I always told myself was the room we stayed in and I saw the reflection of a light in the lake waters. It was the moonrise. I watched it pull up from its nowhere, wishing Michelle was with me and we were lying on the beach. Nothing makes her happier than these marvels of nature. I told myself if we didn't have two kids to stay with I would have ridden back home and grabbed her to join me, but of course, the moment is the moment and you must be there or not because the moon would just be the moon by the time I hustled her out of there, away from her contemptible high school friends and to the beach. With one moon before me and one behind me, I wondered if it saw the reflection and grew curious of this other moon. I watched it edge out of the indigo glow and felt illuminated myself with this simple knowledge that the moon is moving by no effort of its own. But one is caught in an endless orbit between the sun and the earth. Circling again and again. The other will vanish at the edge of the window pane.

I began pedaling harder, leaning in, caught up in the Chicago night, navigating Museum Campus and veering west before Soldier Field. Ready to know what was next. The bike changed my mind all the time. It was as if I were new again to this city, that this place had spun and *voilà*, another site for excavation.

CHAPTER ELEVEN

L eSabre was similar to the bars we spent so much time at when Michelle and I were young. Thursday nights carried a top crowd. The room was full. I knew more faces than I did names and in the low lighting of flickering candles everyone was half in shadows and half illuminated, like each was caught at the threshold of exiting a dark cave into some revelation or another. The heady math rock of Maps & Atlases *You And Me And the Mountain* was on, layering an intellectual trance across the faces and revealing some kinetic edge to the tables and chairs, as if a seat was all it took to activate that tantalizing wellspring of wild energy within each of us. I saw a few eyes glance my way as I walked through the tables towards the bar. I nodded to each, smiling. Some nodded back.

At the far end of the bar, I saw Mona leaning in talking with Jill as she cleaned a few pint glasses. Jill was infatuated with Mona. We all were. I slid into the one empty stool nearby without interrupting them and then tried to catch Mona's attention fumbling with coasters, straws, then finally writing *555-0113 Call Me* on a matchbook and sliding it past the two people between us, who were not amused, landing exactly where she set her beer down. She read it, cocked her head back and laughed, then looked in my eyes, smiling, and I realized I rode all this way simply to feel as good as I did right then.

—I thought I recognized that number.

—The one and only.

—Gene Parmesan, Private Eye. How you doing?

—Grated. How are you?

—Doing well. But my wit's run out on me. If you could help me find it, Detective?

—You still number one Dungeon Master on the west side?

—Good memory. Nope. Got befuddled by this 12-year-old named Terrence when I took my team through the ancient forest without initiating the charm to protect us from malevolent elves. Sucks.

Mona had curly red hair, messy atop her head, an oversized green scarf draped over her white t-shirt and gray knickerbocker pants. She was some sort of tall chimney sweep sitting mischievously on the hearth and behind her kindled something I wanted to understand. Something like the heart of Saturday night. But this was a Thursday and I hadn't listened to Tom Waits in years. Jill interrupted us.

—I just think I need to find something else.

—Nothing is so heavy you can't deal with it, sweetie.

Hug?

—This guy's a bit older than your usual. And he tips like a nun.

Mona guffawed and slapped the bar, blushing and looking at me.

—I'll grab a piece of welfare bread for you on my way out the door next time.

—Don't go buttering your lembas now, old man.

—You've been bartending here longer than I've been in big boy pants.

—I've always thought of you as the underoos type.

Jill had been bartending at LeSabre since the early 90s when Podmajersky developed the block with lofts and gallery spaces. A mean face, grumpy wrinkles across her forehead, sloppy tattoos on her large arms and shoulders, always wearing a green or brown tank top. She could see through me, which at first gave me pause, but although much harsher than my mother, I appreciated her in that way, knowing I wore LeSabre like a grand tortoise shell.

—I come here to be known, Jill, and most mornings when I'm hungover from your stiff drinks, I praise you in my head for keeping me humble.

—You remind me of myself when I was your age. Never wanting a dull moment.

—Is that how you kept your wit so sharp? Dry humor

spread thin across dull moments—ain't life grand.

—Once upon a time, Chicago was a whetstone. You know this, I know this, but Mona and your friend there, none of these kids understand.

Gershwin came up behind me.

—These two are bird songs and then some, right Jill?

—Not mangy enough for my menagerie.

—Satchel has a new sitcom he wants to pitch us. Do a shot with us, Jill.

—Right, I was going to save it for the grand finale, but it just might be one of those nights that starts where it ends.

—Jill quit drinking.

—The pretty ones spill the most secrets.

—Put some water in one then, we'll cheers your sobriety.

—Well Gershwin just punched out my least favorite word.

—Sobriety?

—Cheers.

—Mine is socialist.

—Sober socialists cheersing… might as well castrate Chicgao altogether.

—Booze has been behind a lot of the *umpf* around here.

—Mona, didn't a psychic say you were Lucy Parsons

in a past life?

—She was an anarchist, but yes. I still wonder about that.

—Not believing in reincarnation these days?

—It's something Jill and I were just talking about. Art, all these artists around us—and no revolution in sight.

—Cheers.

—Cheers.

—To sobering up the artists. Jill will lead the way.

—Everything is interesting enough, but no one puts their life on the line. All the narratives set against Lucy and other anarchists as being un-American worked. Now instead of being in a bar full of Americans, we're in a bar full of artists.

—You should come up to my neighborhood and drink at The Anvil with me—plenty of Americans.

—The artists are growing restless—I've got drinks to pour.

—Anarchists, civil rights, beats, hippies, hip hoppers, slackers—we're children of so many movements.

—Mutts.

—No offense to my art school teacher here, but how many do we know with arts degrees? You can't tap into that stream of vitality in an institution financed by war-mongering banks. It's why I dropped out.

—It's why I quit.

—You were thrown out.

—I was thrown out. Much more macho.

—Macho now that is my least favorite word. Not trying to go 0-to-60 feminist on you, but the way we perform masculinity in American culture, I think you could rope it into the same thing I was saying before. We're taught to be American, meaning capitalist, and we're taught to be macho and define our success by how we fair in a capitalist economy.

—I'm lost to know how I should let the world define me.

—Welcome to womanhood. That's part of the feminine condition in our culture.

—This is why I loved and hated your classes, Satchel. Everything was always so abstract. I don't feel macho, don't get lost in any of those insecurities, and I don't feel subjected to American or capitalist narratives. I've just lost the tempo.

—Mona, what about you? I think you both are the same age.

—I'm not sure what age has to do with it, but for me, I've been working with fabric since I was little. It's always held my attention. We all get together here and we all know each other, but still I've just been sad about not having a real community. Everything is transactional—like the way Nina and Wes are sitting there with Tim, direct or not, everything she is saying is about landing a show at his gallery. And I love Bert and Junior down there but they will want me to know about their gig at The Hideout coming up, not that anything will come out of it but a night, maybe a really fun night, but just a night and they want me, you, anyone to be there so they feel, I don't know, like they are successful.

—Not anyone, they want a specific crowd.

—It's all curated.

—Curation.

—Before it was creation. Now it's curation.

—Maybe it's that I never know where my rent money is coming from, and I'm just anxious, but still.

—We're mutts sorting through all the shit our ancestors laid upon us.

—Nobody else gets it but maybe in light of this conversation, you two will. I'm not doing the Thrill Jockey gig, anymore. They asked me to leave.

—Yeah, what's this about Coup de Brew?

—I need to find something.

—But what happened, I don't get it.

—Part of the deal was they wanted me to bring bands in, so I did, right. A couple of them I knew a little too well, and things rekindled, which caused some drama.

—Oh man, so you were?

—Yeah, I was sleeping with a few of them, whatever, it's all messy and I understand, I guess, but I also don't. This is me, right, and this is music, and it's sexy—it really is.

—Oh sweetie, I'm sorry. I hear you. Also, if musicians know you are sleeping with the bands you bring in, it seems like you could be taken advantage of.

—I guess if I lacked integrity then yes, someone could just fuck me and I'd do their album. I thought I had the good faith of everyone there. Maybe I'm just an idiot.

—So it's over?

—I don't want to get caught up in discovering musicians anyway. Everso subtly enhancing their songs into an album. There's so much out there, and what are we aspiring to with all of this? Music or art—any of it.

—Is that why you haven't made an album in a while?

—I mean I've been playing my guitar, coming up with new stuff, it's just how it goes for me, but yes, I think I'm just tired of putting music out there then having to be dragged through making money off of it—that's what the shows and the merch and all that became, or always was, but I had to experience it.

—Why did we go so far with art?

—This reminds me of my new idea for a tv show.

—Let's hear it.

—So it's the same old tune. A brother/sister orphan dance team are so broke that they can't pay the rent and have been evicted from their childhood home. Right around the corner from here in fact. They're forced to busk on the streets and begin scampering with the local urchins and ne'er-do-wells and one day they find a treasure map in a trash can, sending them on adventures across the city night after night which they fill with well-choreographed numbers that charm even the most musical-adverse among us. Meanwhile, their vicious rich uncle follows close behind, promising some inheritance once the legal side of things are handled but really looking to pounce as soon as they uncover the treasure. Season two, he becomes their manager and pimps them across the country.

—Season three?

—All depends on the political climate.

Mona laughed and grabbed my arm smiling. Her golden eyes lit up as she leaned into me. That made me feel good. Made me want to feel that good again.

—Feel like you just summed up my life's story.

—I know he's old but the tequila still takes him where he wants to go.

A nearby table called out to Gershwin. It was Nina and Wes, both friends of his from art school. He laughed, squeezed my shoulder and headed their way. Leaving Mona and I alone.

—How much older than us are you anyways?

—You don't want to get me started on age.

—Well, what do you like talking about?

—New Orleans.

—I've never been. To New Orleans.

—When you do, you might not come back.

—Dangerous?

—Very. And there's strange magic portals, folds in time that slide you back a day, a decade—you never know. But they're inescapable, so basically yeah, you're trapped.

—Like *Quantum Leap*.

—Oh you're a Bakula fan?

—Love Bakula.

—In New Orleans one of the most terrifying stories the locals tell is about a vampire called Bakula Dracula.

—Instead of the slow aching burn of eternal parasitical life, he gets to whoosh off and have a nonlinear menu of historical necks to feast from?

—Yeah and the legend goes each one of us crosses his path at least once in our lifetime. And the only way he can cease the spell of leaping throughout time is if he can be bit by a non-vampire.

—Wouldn't it be something if revolutionaries like Lucy Parsons could spread their anarchy by biting people's necks?

—Or if artists could just skip the making and satisfy their compulsive need to express themselves with a kiss.

—The best art is like a kiss.

—Maybe that's why art is such a visceral deal for the young.

—They way you just said *the young* has got me nervous you might be the Bakula Dracula you speak of. That was creepy.

—I'm thirty-five. Everything I do has a hint of creepiness.

Jill switched the music. I don't think she realized it, but she put on one of Gershwin's albums, the one he wrote when he was in my class at Columbia with some friends from his dorm. They would always invite me to get high with them after class, and the one time I did, they played it for me and I was amazed. They called themselves The Fountain. It was an EP, four songs, and at the time it felt to me like a moment-defining work of art. An encapsulation not a full realization, but the confidence and execution that makes a completely personal creation attractive to anyone deeply interested in youth music, youth sub-culture. Truly from and of the conversations of the Chicago South Loop art students alive around 2008.

I saw a few people looking at him, and if Jill didn't know, they knew. Nina was leaning in with a close intellectual intensity, as she always did with Gershwin. When she began rubbing his arm, Gershwin motioned for me to come over. I got my wallet out and put cash down for our drinks.

But Mona stopped me.

—No, I'll buy.

—That's alright. I got it.

—You're well-respected around here. If people see me drinking with you, my social currency triples. Jill, don't take his money.

—What money? I already told you.

—Alright then. But let me teach you a spell that might be useful for regaining the Dungeon Master title.

—Fucking Terrence, hate that kid.

—You know Gershwin don't you? I mean he was just right here but I wasn't sure.

—You mean Rey Mysterio?

—Come on.

—That's what we call him.

—That's so good. You've gotta hang out with us tonight.

—Alright but I get to be the one to unmask him.

Chapter Twelve

Nina made room for us at their table. Wes didn't look up except to look at the entrance, which he was sketching in his journal by the light of the red-textured glass candleholder.

—You two know Satchel? I think you took his writing class at Columbia.

—Hey.

—I don't think I did but yeah, hey.

—That's right. And, of course, Mona.

—How'd it go with Tim?

—Maybe showing at Tim Tal early fall.

—Nina did you study painting?

—And art history which got me into criticism.

—She was just telling me about the write-up she did on Arwen.

—I know Arwen.

—We all know Arwen?

—Gersh, you need to go see her exhibit—it's not like you'd think. I feel she knows your expectations and uses them to become the negative space. It's pleasing, and displeasing. It's playful, like you have to be able to notice your experience of the painting in order to experience the painting.

—You're totally right. She's so clever.

—Her forms are staunch. Iconic.

—Quintessential.

—Where's it up?

—Trevor's apartment.

—What's he call that space?

—The Factory.

—Lame.

—Old guy calling it out.

I peered over Wes' entrenched arm to see his drawing. It was an impression of the room. The air buzzed with precise tiny curly-q's compounding densely into the shadows. The faces, angular and active, expressing lonely monstrous selves. Checkmarks formed the tables, drinks, candles, and bar. He was rubbing his thumb over the lines he'd drawn on the other side of the entrance, smearing them into street blurs of haunted nights. I noticed the people passing had mounds of winter clothes on. The effect was as if their bodies were dissolving away by the cold winds, their faces and elbows worn through, revealing bone. Yet outside, it was a warm spring night.

—How's everything at Thrill Jockey, Gersh?

—You know, things went south there.

—Weren't you here with her the other week?

—They were all really cool. Still got some figuring out

to do personally, I guess.

—Are you just done with music?

Hearing this, it was the only time Wes looked up and said anything.

—His album is on. It exists. What else is there to do?

—Just having some troubles and they threw me out.

—I'll never forget when you got tossed from Columbia. Our friends all wanted to leave with you.

—Why didn't you?

Wes looked back down to his sketch.

—Two years of debt piled up, I guess.

—Hey, all good now. I went on tour, met some others. I get it now.

—You all should've left.

—Says the art teacher paid by our tuition.

—The more I taught at arts colleges, the more I told students they did not need to go to arts college. It delays the inevitable.

—Giving up and finding square work?

—I know a few who haven't made anything for months but still tell themselves they haven't quit. Jobs, though, they're working. Not like they're just spongers.

—Yeah while all of us who are still at it are getting government checks.

—I heard Obama worked with Podmajersky on buying

up all these buildings.

—Fuck this conversation.

—What I meant was committing to art and figuring it out by yourself. That's the inevitable turn an artist's life must take.

—Well, Professor, maybe you're right. Maybe your students just never committed.

—That's the thing, you were different, Gershwin. You had it figured out early.

—Figured out? Listen, I don't want to be a part of false promises. A label puts out your record, you go on tour, if you're lucky get good reviews, and you come home broke. Maybe people know you and think wow, he made something cool, but mostly people don't know you and you're just floating along wondering if the next album will get you there.

—Get you where?

—I have no clue. In my experience there's no *there* to get to. It's not a community anymore, it's a business.

—Enough money, good opportunities that don't waylay your life, and friends who are doing it with you. That's the artist's dream.

—You've got to commit. You can't live all the lives— you've got to commit to the one.

—I feel like I'm reading your comments at the bottom

of my poems. You're not listening to me. When people have to stop being people because they have a specific job and need to now be the job description which human resources wrote for them, I mean, it's the opposite—I'm committed to music, but too much.

—My comments didn't help?

—I've got something set up with Mick tonight. What would help is if you came with me.

—These breweries, man, I don't trust them.

—All you Gen-Xers don't trust jack shit.

—True.

—What's your problem with breweries?

—We saw it with cafes. I was there throwing bricks at the Starbucks at 6 Corners. Now it's the corporate bar. They take over our cultural spaces.

—Maybe I just want my job to be my job and my music to be my music.

—Gershwin, maybe Satch is right. I've got a few friends who said the same thing and they just stopped making stuff, got sucked into the people they were around.

—And why is Mick so hellbent on hiring you?

—Why did Thrill Jockey want me? I'm not blind— they know I'll bring people in.

—You've got a beautiful energy and people want that around. Just make sure and do what you want to do with your time while you're alive. Be ready to suffer the consequences, but be bold and go straight at it.

—Let's just hit up Coup de Brew, talk to Mick and see what's what.

—Before that student-and-teacher field trip, do you two want to go see Sienna and Mark with me?

—Is that the bread backyard?

—Every other Thursday. The oven they built is something.

—Sure.

—It's in Humboldt right?

—On Humboldt but up a little in Palmer Square.

—Stop by Gladys' on the way?

—Where is that?

—Hubbard Street Lofts, beneath Ukrainian Village.

—Warehouses and stuff.

—Don't forget about Jill.

—Oh that's right. She wanted me to stick around.

—Find out for me what it feels like to be fifty.

—Jill's fifty?

—She told me that after she closes up tonight, she is going to burn off every anxiety she's ever been plagued with.

—What does that mean?

—I guess there's some ritual taking place called the

Dislodge.

—Is that what you two were talking about?

—Yeah. I want to go with her but she said bring something heavy. I got confused. And worried. It all sounds cryptic.

—Hinting at suicide?

—I'll meet you outside.

—Yeah.

CHAPTER THIRTEEN

It wasn't until I walked out that I remembered Wes, and I looked back to see he hadn't moved from his spot at our table. How impressed I was at that moment. He hadn't bothered with social niceties, chit-chat, our ramblings. He glanced up and met my eyes. I waved and he smiled, his hand not stopping its tiny gestures of details, only tensing and hurrying while never looking down from my face. I wanted to give him something, but what did I have? Too late to douse him in words, too incomprehensible to rush in and embrace him. His eyes still in mine, I took each index finger and drew a frame in the air between us, and then began to fill it in with a sketch of a bicycle that I then began to blow upon as if it was the wind that moved it. I saw it as an animation now and began to sketch all the things out that night: a moon above, the waves crashing, people hugging, crying, drinking, paying money, playing instruments on the sidewalks beneath the buildings of a city that was never intended to be Chicago, never intended to exist, but only to serve as a gift to him, an affirmation of his unadulterated commitment to do, to try, to be.

Mona walked over wheeling her bike.

—He grew up near here, on the Southside.

—Let's hope he never finds his way up north. The air

up there might be too thin for his peace of mind.

—You rode all the way down here?

—I'll always ride all the way down here, no matter how far north I go.

—Okay, Riddler. Be the Robin to my Batman.

—To the bat cave!

—First I'm going to go pee in the alley over there. Don't look.

—Righty-o, I'll just tend to the bat phone.

Michelle had texted a few times.

—*Everyone is asking about you, saying they wish you were here.*

—*I know things are hard right now but I really needed this.*

—*Miller told me to tell you ruff, ruff!*

I replied.

—*Kiss those cuties on the head for me. Hope all is well.*

—*Just got done eating. How is your night?*

—*Always great to be down here—these are my people.*

—*We're your people too!*

—*Three of you.*

—*I know, I know. Maybe there's some good news though. Can you call?*

—*Let's discuss tomorrow.*

—*Chris and Fred have some ideas, in case you decide not*

to go to law school.

    —That you all were talking about me is hard to stomach.

    —People are always talking. Doesn't mean you have to let them in.

    —Got it. But I like letting people in. Just not those two.

    —Well I won't even mention the job they brought up.

    —Consider it mentioned.

    —Unintentional!

    —I know. I love you. Thanks for being the best.

    —The best around.

    —Nobody could ever take you down.

Chapter Fourteen

Riding down 18th Street rapid hand drums were beating at Blue Island, the streets a mix of drunks, junkies, families on stoops, artist-dressed youth, Mexican proprietors. I saw a sprinkling of tight-lipped UIC college kids, tentatively inching through the street like they were entering the cold lake waters. I questioned the aged disrepair, postulating the surfaces had been weathered purposefully by developers—the aesthetically charming patinas had been allowed to remain by design. A brokedown storefront could no longer be known simply as such—we had moved into the age of curation; Mona was right. Authenticity had become a disguise, an affect.

We headed north towards the train yards and hospitals and expressway. These barricades of inner city development. For bikers, Damen Avenue was an unlit stretch of danger that included a block-long, pitch-black tunnel under the train yards. No bike lane, the roads crumbling and potholed as the drivers sped up behind us, honking, flashing lights, then roaring past. I nervously wondered who it was that drove between these neighborhoods—drinkers between bars, *Call of Duty* gamers, unlicensed immigrants, developers on scouting missions, drug dealers on their way to West

Town, lovers of slurpees, chain smokers. I could feel the cars mount and throttle me, splaying my body across the grease dripping cement columns. As I prayed for my life, promising I would never ride this underpass again, I heard Gershwin let out a *yelp*, and Mona replied with a *yawp* that colored the chamber with a burst of levity. How heavy I had become, how dire. And I reversed my prayer, instead asking if allowed to survive that I may lighten up, float by the grace of the sunward energies.

When we made it to the other side, Mona cruised up and smiled, settling right in front of me. Her long legs, her radiant hips.

—Hey Professor, is that Columbia's graduating class of 1985?

I looked ahead and saw a crowd of old folks gathering on the street corner near the UIC hospital. A few women rolled tanks of oxygen behind, men adjusted their dialysis bags as they looked behind us for an oncoming bus. Decades of hammering upon these bodies as they've traveled the iron city. The convenience store sustenance and airs of industry. These the blacksmith's creations. I could only see their mangled postures and bandages, but I hoped inside they each had found a shape to take which generated their dignity. As the bus pulled up, the beep of the hydraulic lift lowering a wheelchair off, the dim bodies lit up with the fluorescent glow of the CTA, carriage of the fellaheen doom. Every night in the city's forge the blacksmith commands the livery onward as the driver lifts his hands manacled by the reins. What dark horses, snarling as they trot eyeball to eyeball beneath our harness. How could they ever come to be known? I closed my eyes and conjured sharp instruments made of elven magic and wished them upon the world if only for a glimpse of their potential to unbind us all.

My tire hopped the curb and I saw the impending building in time, skidding to a halt.

—Satchel—watch out!

—We should give them our bikes!

Gershwin whipped by, and he gave a tug on Mona's belt loop. She shrieked and chased after him, crossing over the expressway, which once upon a time tore these neighborhoods apart to allow suburbanites easy access to their jobs. I watched them go, the bus passing by dangerously close with breakneck velocity, and all I could think to do was get back on and pedal with a parallel speed. Feeling like the Road Runner speeding down Damen, I looked up again and again expecting to see Wile E .Coyote in some floating apparatus preparing an anvil to drop upon my head. I passed Malcolm X City College, parking lots, and the United Center, all surrounded by remnants of neighborhoods, beautiful and disrupted Victorian three-flats of Madison. The Green Line flew by overhead but did not stop. The Metra glided away smoothly to Schaumburg.

Chapter Fifteen

We turned and rode through three blocks of warehouses and light industry to Hubbard Street Lofts, where one of Gershwin's friends, Gladys, had opened a gallery space for poetry and surrealist art. We hung our bikes next to the rest, Mona and Gershwin shared a cigarette, I put in a piece of Nicorette gum, and we made our way to the entrance.

We passed through a long, cavernous hallway of metal floors and timbered ceilings. There was a freight elevator, but we decided to take the stairs. At the second-floor landing we could hear loud music, dance beats, and a woman ran past us screaming excitedly, then down the stairs and to who knows where.

—Who's on this floor?

—Narrative Metrics, mostly. Some sort of branding agency, or whatever.

—What happened to all the artist lofts?

—Galdys is holding on. But it's expensive.

—Anything else?

—Next to them there's a kickass cultish group who collaborates on performance art throughout the city.

—That's sexy. Are they making all the noise?

—I don't know.

—I heard an arts podcast has moved in, too. Bummed About Style, I think.

—You two want to check out whatever this is we're hearing?

—Nope.

—Not me.

—Okay. I'm gonna.

—See you up there.

The boisterousness spilled down the hallway as I turned the corner out of the staircase. Two people stood at the doorway to the loft smoking cigarettes, their eyes lit up and talking. Dressed identically, and each had a hand fully-vested in the other's long sculpted reddish-brown beard. The arms were ripped off their plaid shirts, unbuttoned down to their belly buttons. Black leather jackets tied around their waists. Long chains between their belt buckle and back pocket hung far down their white jeans. Shiny black boots, unlaced, like they had only just slipped them on to come out and smoke. The talking didn't stop as I stood there taking them in.

—Absolutely, you know how unbelievable and she had a tooth.

—A tooth like a razor or what?

—Two sharp edges spilling around the skin, I don't want that. I know you know.

—Let's ask him.

And they eyed me.

—Do you want to come in?

—Is this the marketing firm?

—*Alright alright alright.*

—You all podcasting?

— No, my man, no pods—just dad bods.

—That's hilarious.

—I will. Who's inside?

—Come in and see.

—What's happening?

—Pharmacy hours.

—That the DJ?

—Blood beats man.

—Let me guess. You two are Gemini, right?

They giggled.

—Quick survey.

—Shoot.

—How happy are you with your entrance.

—1 to 5.

—4.

—Where did you hear about this space?

—Someone penned it on the wall at Phyllis' Musical Inn.

—Tight.

—Thank you, sir.

—I love these old cats.

I walked in, saw they were playing Twister, and almost immediately walked back out.

At least ten mats, five or more people on each. The music was not from a DJ, but an iPad plugged into a speaker box: Miss Kitten. Having gone to several raves in the 00s, I knew her music. *Lick lick, suck suck, that's the way I like to fuck.* People were miming these actions to each other and giggling as they maneuvered their bodies on the mats.

At first glance, it seemed to be a sea of MTV-era hipsters. But as I walked along the walls of the huge loft, I noticed the misfitting t-shirts, too baggy or too tight, the still rigid jean jackets filled with band patches that didn't gel—Pantera, Hall and Oates, Michael Jackson, Lungfish, Metallica, Fugazi, Phil Collins. The pants were tight, but new and creased. Women wore leggings, sweatshirts, electric colors—sure signs of being in their early twenties around 2005, when American Apparel hit the scene. Almost everyone in Converse high tops or Doc Martens.

But there was one person dressed entirely separate from the crowd, alone and looking through the window. I grabbed a can of RC Cola from the vintage Coke machine that reminded me of the one in the Duds n' Suds where I used to do my laundry and wandered in their direction. They wore a red and blue tunic. The yellow and green sleeves billowed and ended with scalloped cuffs. Green tights. Yellow shoes. A drooping broad-brimmed hat.

—No theme?

—Where?

—Everybody else is from different eras.

—Yes. Like the fire escape and the curtains.

—The irony of liking Fugazi and Phil Collins wasn't a thing back then.

—You're right. We used to stay on brand. Now, we're a bit more fluid.

—Brand was a four-letter word when I first moved to Chicago.

—The good 'ol days.

—You might be the most twisted of all the Twisters.

—You are scoring quite high on the language skills portion of the test. Did you complete the survey?

—What sort of work goes on here?

—We don't use the W word.

—Any chance you are hiring? Obama is about to kick me off unemployment.

—This isn't an interview.

—What sort of view is it?

They turned from the window to look in my eyes.

—What's your jam, old-timer?

—Cities. Horses, too—I dream of horses.

—And?

—Words.

—What good are words when you can ride horses through cities?

—Mystically prodding them. Stretching them out across a city and watching them snap to reveal the other side.

—How are you at floor games?

—I'm willing.

—I can see your pupils' reflection in the window across the alley.

—I try not to be so forthcoming.

—My name is Marseilles.

—Satchel.

—We're a collaborative. You must know the difference. Spiritually. Economically. Currently, we do have an opening.

—Wonderful. Would I need a law degree to get the gig?

—Who's laws would you be doctoring?

—Right.

—We need one more person on mat F, below the chandelier.

Not turning away from the window, they pointed, and I floated in that direction, stopping beneath the dim huddle of lights. There I found a heavy metal rocker, a Flashdancer, Screech from *Saved By the Bell*, and two of the Ramones, one of which had the spinner in her lap. All attractive in their twenties, and I quickly became self-conscious about my bald spot.

Standing behind me, Marseilles shot a glitter cannon across the room as Frankie Knuckles' "Your Love" came on. They looked my way and cheered. The bicameral clash of synthetic loop and beat. Screech grabbed my arm to pull me in.

Before I knew it I had my left foot on green, left hand on red, my right elbow on blue which put my face near the ass of a pair of stone-washed Cherokee jeans that kept that vintage clothes storage locker smell. The game moved forward but I couldn't manage any more spins, so I stayed positioned like that. Many nights when I get in bed I am met with the echoes of the previous night's dreams. The same occurrence happened there on the Twister mat as I grew lost searching through my grandmother's attic, bent over and tossing Christmas ornaments and wool sweaters up in the air, stirring up a musty chaos of tchotchkes and crackling magazine cut-outs, papers everywhere, stretched clothing, spilling moth balls and evading cob webs in search of my father's baseball cards. Until I felt a hand rubbing the top of my head.

—Whoa, what's this peachy soft glittery spot.

A warmth gathered above my eyes at the same time as a panic ran down my spine.

—I want to touch it, too.

Another hand which brought more warmth. I tried to peer up to see who rubbed my bald spot, but I was committed to my pose. And the touches were soft, comforting, not a trace of mockery. Simply a human touching a human and all the good that comes from that rushed through my nerve-endings dampening any uptight reaction. The warmth melted away my panic and a loose heat spilled through every inner working of my mind and body.

My eyes opened when I heard a slug of drool hit the Twister mat. I saw it continue falling through the yellow dot which was the opening of a cord that traveled through the crust and water and rock and ore of the earth until it reached the core. With each new hand that came to rub my head, a buzz of love—what else can I call it?— continued to circulate through my body and my thoughts, dislodging the shadows that had gathered and become stuck inside me. And I watched them spill from my being, following that droplet of spittle through the tube to its end where the center of the earth burned and disintegrated these weights I was unaware I had been carrying.

Quickly after the last hand lifted from my head, the team of bodies pushed into my space and I softly tumbled to the mat. They had begun touching each other in this same caressing way, tenderly squeezing every inch of each now half-naked body.

I crab-walked off the mat. Ice Cube's "It Was a Good Day" came on. I noticed my heart, a quick pump of blood, as I looked up and saw that the walls were dry erase boards full of a day's work—logos, slogans, lines and sketches. Were these the marketers? This must be their work, their means to the end game of discovering brand narratives, designing information architectures, and transferring life into virtual spaces. How similar, I realized, to the rituals of artists in the vein of Rimbaud and Jim Morrison, deranging their senses to deprogram their hegemonic indoctrination and experience the unknown. I grew heavy again, paranoid that I had just been branded by the vanguard of creatives who would usher in a monstrous system of disembodied social currency, creating digitized prisons for our commodified existences. A roomful of hideous Orcs in mid-transformation, and they were on the clock.

As I got up Marseilles gathered all their nostalgic

cultural garments, strewn about in their rush to disrobe, and began to toss them into a bonfire. The naked bodies of the futurists, I thought as I hurried away.

The twins giggled to see me leaving.

—No more Twister, *brother*?

—Going upstairs.

—*Do the right thing.*

—*Ya'll come back now you hear?*

Their tone of voice betrayed the confusion of their irony: equal parts satire and parody. An instant self-effacement.

—*Have yourself a merry little Christmas.*

—*Whatchyou talkin'bout, Willis!*

—I only slaw redacto, but in my head, I'm sequestered.

—What's that from?

—Fucking old guys are hilarious.

—Arcane *in the membrane.*

I walked upstairs anticipating the derangement to subside.

CHAPTER SIXTEEN

The energy of Gladys' gallery hushed my haywire mind. Like scaling the frozen waves of Lake Michigan locked by winter's hold, I centered my posture knowing how slippery and hard a room full of Chicgao artists like these could be.

Avoiding eye contact, I headed directly to the apothecary bureau where the booze had been set up. Clear Dixie cups, I poured warm white wine to the top, found a wall to lean on and lifted my eyes to take in the room. The crowd was dirty debonair. Serious about their artistry. Not a gregarious soul among the pile.

I saw Mona caught up in a conversation near the large window overlooking smokestacks and train yards, and I wanted to grab her by the waist and stir up talk of all the things we saw through the glass, all we wished we saw. I wanted to make her laugh and smile, but she was caught up listening to a few others, two of which I saw around often but whenever I had tried saying *hi*, as I do, they would not respond but for a curious glance. Strange to me, not to acknowledge one another.

I did a once-around the loft, but I couldn't find Gershwin. The paintings were by an artist named Vulcan. Naked figures in cityscapes, men and women, either falling as if the floor had dropped out from under them or rising to the heavens. Somewhere in the body of those crashing through the floor was a weight, a large object that appeared to be the gravitational extra that was pulling them down. Those who ascended were defecating and urinating large chunks, I did not know, and their faces were euphoric as they shot up towards some celestial realm.

On the wall was an artist's statement, which I read in earshot of Mona's laughter.

The Vanquishing of The Anvil
Created by Vulcan

If one goes to the trouble of devising a philosophy of life in their twenties, then one will surely begin to choke on it in their thirties.

Initially, turning thirty isn't so horrible. It is a dramatic turn of the dial, but you can still wear your 20s like a costume. Thirty-one is troublesome, but that beautiful delusion of youth is still in the bloodstream. Not fully potent, but you still expect that what you are witnessing is your own private Idaho.

Thirty-two, chances are depression has set in.

Thirty-three you hope the Christian God will take you from this planet like he did his son. Or, that you have the gusto of Henry Miller to move to Paris and solidify your artistry.

At age thirty-four you have become an encyclopedia of arachnids—you know every spider and every web, and watching teevee sounds so much better than it once did. Why not, you think, watch a million episodes of quality storytelling over the on-setting winter.

With turning thirty-five came the realization that we each swallow our homegrown anvil. One's only hope is to have devised the necessary acids in the stomach to dissolve it before you die. Because if you die with this anvil in your stomach you will drop to hell. But if you can break it up and pass it through your system, painful like pissing stones, then heaven awaits you. I believe this, I believe it all and know it, too. I am thirty-six and here is the dissolution of my anvil.

I barely made it through these pieces. Six years I spent working on this. In the beginning it was a different project. It was beautiful but not real. It was idyllic pastures of poppy plants. Gauguin-like shacks in the not too far distance. Golden bodies in the Elysian Fields of philosophical hedonism. For two years I kept adding more wildlife and going back over the huts with different colors until I woke up one day and noticed how badly I had blurred the figures and the form into a palette of browns. I loved those browns; I would stare at them for hours and days. I would tell people no, that I was not available to be with them, that I was detained, and then I would go home or stay home in my studio staring at those browns. I started calling in sick once every other week, then more often.

Finally, I began to paint on top of those browns. I manipulated them, replicated them, and arranged them in different ways that gave me pleasure, if only momentarily. Soon after this, I lost my job. That was three years ago. I have worked since then, but only in the most menial capacities, special thanks to unemployment benefits.

The job I had was as a writer for the Chicago Tribune. They became dissatisfied with my appearance, I believe, and the glances I afforded my coworkers. Also, they went bankrupt, and the arts section I wrote for was slashed from the budget. During these past three years I have lost several friends to data disease and doctorate school. It has been sad. I almost killed myself—life felt that insignificant. In earnest, I asked the most significant question: *Why continue to live when life is like being some nutcracker stuck on repeat?* Those mornings I would awake and feel a vacuousness that surely extended from the stretch of nothingness between Saturn's rings and moons. There was neither subjecthood nor a system of cycling rhythms; I was just a balloon inflated by my breath.

I had a wife. We are now divorced. I have children; I have never had a dime to pay them. People hate me; I hate myself, or I did, until I finished these works.

When I turned 34, the manipulation of brown became an arduous study of gray, and a year later there it was: The Anvil. Glowing on my canvas as I was choking on my own. Instantaneously, I knew what must be done from there. Tonight in this room, you are experiencing The Vanquishing of The Anvil.

The people in this series of paintings live their fates thusly.

This anvil that you must swallow feels like drowning; you will not drown, you will not die, let it take you down, follow it down; become a more complex structure than the elemental simplicity you envisioned in your youth. Young at heart is for the weak soul. Transform, this is just transformation.

Visit me to discuss more, I am alive and well in Baltimore.

But he wasn't in Baltimore. He was sitting on a throne in the corner with his legs spread, wearing an extravagant red robe lined in gold that folded and draped in his lap. A gold crown atop his head like an emptied acorn filled with his long white hair which ended in pigtails and a beard dyed blue at the goatee. People came and spoke with him but he never stood up, only leaned in to take sips of white wine from an elaborate straw that looked like the mast of a ship. When he shifted his weight, I could see there were two smaller people mixed up in his garment, that I was sure, but I could not tell if they were privately tying a restraint around his ankles or were freeing him from the cords and ribbons. He did not look down to acknowledge them in any way.

I felt connected to him. Someone so similar to me. This was the beauty of art, I thought, how it shows we are not alone. This is the power in confession. I wanted to start a conversation with him, to connect and maybe to find my answer. So I made my way in his direction.

—How light do you feel?

—Why, just look. My shoulders are brushing with the loft timbers.

—I see you over here and think yes, the paintings and the artist statement are something, but truly the product of your art is you.

—Astute.

—So what now? The 40s are coming.

—I'll simply stay in this clearing, nothing more. Eye what I eye, feel what I feel, create or not. You surely notice there's nothing that's pushing on me, nothing that is tying me down, my only tug is from the heavens.

—Heaven?

—Levity! Up!

—I'm a writer.

—Poor thing.

—And every book I have written has only grinded me down to a more ridiculous pulp. I couldn't put myself back together as I previously was if I tried. And no notoriety, no money, just more books out there that no one reads.

—You would prefer to be Humpty Dumpty? Everyone knows him but it doesn't illuminate his situation.

—Good point.

—I'm guessing you have kids.

—Perceptive.

—Your tattoos.

—Right, those are for them.

—Kids cost time. Cost money. Cost unity. No gestalt once you have procreated.

—The worst is I feel like I'm selling my kids on a vision of life that will only put them in the same predicament as me.

—As everyone. Differences are only narratives projected atop the browns and grays.

—Okay.

—Their lives are not about you.

—No?

—You should free your parents of the same guilt. Don't blame them for where you are.

—Parent issues. I haven't considered that.

—We don't know how to ask for what we need until our 20s, so how could your parents anticipate your *you* and provide what you tell yourself you need?

—By knowing themselves. And opening up to their kids about their private conversations of self. That way they can get a head start on the baggage of being which gets heaped upon them.

He fidgeted some and I saw the fabric moving near his ankles. He strained to speak.

—This is a high expectation.

His eyes blinked rapidly and began to water as his lips tightened.

—I'm guessing your mom didn't buy you that robe.

—Neither did my children.

He strained forward for a sip from the long straw he held in his hand and looked beyond me, over my right shoulder.

—As a parent, I wonder if having children provokes and jars loose foundational anxieties we keep smothered in our subconscious. Those deep architectures of fear and taboo built in our infancy and throughout our childhood. Like monsters smoked out from under the beds, we can either let them rule and rear our children, or we can deal with them once and for all.

Veins lit up above his white beard to his eyes which were about to burst. He would have bitten through a tree branch if it was between his teeth. He responded to me but he spoke to the little ones between his legs.

—Patricide will only leave you uncovered in the howling winds.

I heard the commotion of the crowd. I turned around and there on top of a chair stood Gershwin, gathering a small group and pointing to different paintings as he talked wildly to the room full of artists who seemed stuck on pause. Seeing him dynamic in this frozen sea, I felt a shift. Moods, I saw in that moment how beautiful our moods are. They should be performed, and we should allow space for the moods of others. We need to let it all pour through. We need to make room for the outpouring of others. We need to sing and we need to receive song. Everyone I noticed in that room, in so many rooms of my Chicago life, seemed paralyzed by outside energies which distorted the sound of their own voices, perverting their powers into shelters. Confidence, I went on in my head, who stole the artist's confidence? But there Gershwin stood taller than everyone, stirring up the laconic room into a frenzy, and I swelled with pride.

But I was wrong. The commotion was not for his song.

Across the loft, emerging out of a curtain came a line of nuns. Each nun rose above the crowd, either on stilts or by puppetry, gangling forward with slow intentional steps, donning self-fashioned gowns covered by a robe gathered at their shoulders. Some so tall they made a show of touching the ceilings.

The crowds' shoulders grew larger, barely parting for the nun's procession.

The tallest of them all was some sort of puppetry built up from the wearer's shoulders. The blue floor-length gown was radiant when visible beneath the sparkling red and green robe lined with gold rope. It swooshed from side-to-side with each dramatic step forward. Most spectacular of all was the nun's wimple which was intricately shaped into two golden horns. The golden veil down, concealing the face of the puppet.

As she walked, out dropped eggs from her back.

One dropped at Mona's feet and she immediately bent over to snatch it. I saw her mesmerized and smiling as her eyes teared up with joy. Next to her the others cringed, puckering up their faces. Gershwin stood tall on his chair but looking up at the spectacle, grinning, chuckling, one arm raised in triumph the other hand stroking his beard. Below him people were squinting as if they just couldn't see it clearly, pursing their lips and crossing their arms.

I finished off my dixie cup of wine as they approached me, ready to be knocked one way or another. The head nun's swooshing robe seemed to be swallowing up individuals from the crowd. Seeing the tallest was the last nun from the curtain, I peered through the crowd to see if anything followed. But I caught a whiff before I saw anything. Frankincense and myrrh quickly intoxicated the room. Behind the nuns were fourteen minions wearing nothing but intricate silk kimonos, brilliantly shining reds, greens, blues, and gold. They circled a coffin which they carried with one hand, the other hand holding a cigar which they puffed and puffed filling the room with frankincense and myrrh.

When the head nun came near, I looked up and could see below the veil. The pale complexion, no gender, no youth. A golden crown towering from the forehead upwards. The eyes met mine and the room went dark as the robe fell upon my body, so soft and so heavy to pull me in.

I was not alone. Dunbar, a poet and a friend since I arrived in Chicago, was fumbling with the folds of the gown looking for a way out. Gray curls and beard, he wore a white t-shirt with yellowed armpits, green suspenders holding his wrinkled black slacks up over his round belly. Considerably older than me, he'd been able to keep to the task of writing in a way I always admired, never entertaining the notion of being and doing anything else. Bands would have him read poems to open up their sets, and he'd sell his books at those shows or pedal them on Milwaukee Avenue in Wicker Park. People said he'd been injured and received disability payments from his union—there were many theories, but no one knew of any work he did other than poetry.

—I think I'm trapped inside a nun's womb.

—Dunbar!

—Who needs this rebirth jazz? Not me, man.

—You see Gerswhin?

—Who's that you all are with? Red-heads make me nervous.

—What happens now we're inside the nun?

—I've got no clue—I'm not Catholic.

—Poverty, chastity, obedience.

—I've got one of the three down. Any horses come in to rectify your impoverished and chaste life?

—Ha! This morning I was a photo finish away from winning a year's salary.

—You could spend the rest of the year riding your bike around and reading books and shit.

—I guess.

—I've been thinking about your situation since I met you up at The Anvil the other week.

—Yeah, that night I was pretty low.

—You've been down a long time, my friend. We gotta get you to see the light of day.

—I need to let the law school know tomorrow.

—Well, you were right about there being no real writers there—those company men-types depress me. Continue your journey south.

—Amen to that.

—I'm forty-four and I don't know, I think this Vulcan guy needs to amp up the mellow and tone down the dramatic.

—Dunbar, no way you're a year younger than fifty-five.

—Once forty-four, always forty-four. You'll understand—it's a peach of an age.

In an instant, we fell out the back of the robe and to the ground. Like the eggs. I looked up to see a minion offering us each a kimono. Others who had similarly been ingested were taking off their clothes and putting one on. Then grabbing hold of the handles on the coffin. Dunbar never batted an eye. Once naked I saw how weak he was. His limp shoulders, belly flaps, hairy crotch—track marks along both upper thighs.

I denied the request. But soon another minion came up behind the first, beseeching me to take the kimono. I looked around and no one else who had come through the robe was saying no.

Still, I denied again.

The procession went forward as I backed out to the rear. More of the crowd tumbled out the nun's habit as they made their way through the room. When Mona rolled out, she said yes. Soon after, I saw Gershwin accepting the kimono, too. When they came to me with the third request to don the kimono, I heard the final movement of the parade. Roosters. Live roosters. Crowing and proceeding to peck at each other and rush throughout the room.

I shook my head.

Right then, Michelle texted. I walked out to respond, letting the ceremony conclude without me.

—*You okay?*

I was okay.

—*Yes, still with Gershwin. Just found Dunbar.*

—*Say hey for me. Coming home?*

—*At some point.*

—*I thought we had something to talk about?*

—*Ok. Well don't wait up, I'm not sure.*

—*Not sure…*

—*When I'll be home.*

—*You okay?*

—*That's what we need to talk about.*

—*Right.*

—*Kids sleeping?*

—*Soundly.*

—*Love you guys.*

—*We love you too … no matter what.*

—*Thanks. What else could I want but that?*

As I hit send, I realized how that could be read as sarcasm. Not my intention, but I couldn't deny it was in my mind as I typed. I left a question hanging and I wondered if subconsciously I was trying to put the onus on Michelle. Make her answer or be the answer to my question of father in tatters or intact.

Back in their clothes, Gershwin, Dunbar, and Mona waved to me from the door. Onward.

Chapter Seventeen

We traipsed back through the building and out to our bikes. We headed west on Hubbard and immediately saw Tommy's Grill where I used to go to and write when I could not sleep. I would walk the streets until something opened up, and usually a little after 5 a.m. I would end up there. The regulars were blue collar men working nearby in the warehouses and scrap yards. They put off a depressed air like their life was not worth living. Monstrosities of spirit forged by back-breaking work in demeaning foot-on-neck systems. When I looked at them, they made me feel ungrateful. As if they were weaponized by their exploitation, and I owed them respect for the pain they carried. I was in awe of the generations of broken backs which built this place, and on those mornings, I learned to offer my respect by bearing my own deformities in plain sight, shuffling into the diner sleepless, listless, overfilled with the hours and days I spent walking and watching and writing. Questioning my sanity yet in love with the morning as people gathered and ate and grew warm with coffee, signaling the nightmare was over and the day's rhythms would dance all of us back to an innocence once known.

I took the lead and turned for my favorite way through

Ukrainian Village. Past Michelle's old apartment on Walton, up Hoyne to Cortez and then west. Nighttime in these streets could wash the monotonous grid of predictability from the city and set you feeling lost in another country and another time. Hulking three-flats with brick front porches at each level met by the canopy of catalpa trees. The copper green spires of St. Nicholas church, always visible over the buildings. A darkness built along each street but was then interrupted by the yellow wash of streetlights at each intersection. Moving through this neighborhood unlocked something in my imagination, allowing me to access a larger part of myself. I rode slowly, and nobody seemed to mind.

We passed the Empty Bottle at Western. The Ruff La Las headlined with three other bands beneath: Sunset Orc, Jersey Tom's Masquerade, and Killing It—all bands I knew nothing about.

Once we hit Humboldt Park—an expansive, fractured checkerboard of grass, ponds, paths, bushes, and trees— we headed north until North Avenue, and I led us west wanting to show them the newspaper I worked at years ago, though it was off course.

The nighttime glare across the windshields, momentary slashing beams of light off rims in the intersections. All of the dust kicked up by the #56 bus in the street light.

The sidewalks spotted black by gummy stains, each store front sealed by metal curtains. The Cicero horse track in the air. I knew right then that North Avenue went forever west. I treated it as I treated my life, longing for it yet not willing to exhaust it too soon. I knew it went forever and I wanted to know how forever felt. The *panaderias*, *carnecerias*, Central Park. Pulaski. The haze of dust, *Puertorriquenas*, mustaches intertwined with stop lights, an American artist strutting in rags, overwrought old-time minds—I never knew if what I looked at was devastating or gorgeous but I had spent years strumming each street with my eyes, listening for the answers in my heart.

I spun around the poles underneath the corner building turrets, wondering if Gershwin and Mona were still behind me, but not wanting to look, overwhelmed by such a strong desire to be lost—a compulsive need to shoot off into each neighborhood, to know everything about the city and be everywhere all at once, adding block after block and detail after detail to the street that runs the course of my mind.

—Satchel, you got quiet there.

—We were shouting to you to turn around.

—I didn't hear.

We had reached the house with the bread oven on Humboldt Boulevard. It was near the end of the night for them, but there was still a dozen or so people sitting around the fire, drinking beer, standing and talking. We locked our bikes to the hundred-year-old waist-high cast iron fence. Gershwin stared up at the mansion and looked to Mona.

—What a gem.

—Wait till you have the bread.

People looked our way as we came in, saying nothing and carrying on in their conversations. They weren't necessarily older than the artists at LeSabre, but they carried a jarring air which undercut their youth, as if they had stepped onto a conveyor belt and absentmindedly forgotten to step back off. Dunbar said it best.

—These are the ones who got lost in a closet trying on their uncles and aunties clothes.

—You two. Be nice.

—How do you know this crowd, Mona?

—From the galleries. These are the people who actually buy art.

—No but see, they forgot to undress.

—Dunbar is definitely on the prowl.

—Maybe to some I seem like a guy who is just staring, man, but really I'm making sense of it all.

—Here she comes.

Sienna, the host and breadmaker, floated our way

—Guys, guys, guys—you made it.

—Sienna!

—Hi! And hi. I

—Hi, sweetie.

—Mona, your hugs are better than a warm bakery.

—How's the night turning out?

—Maybe our best set-up yet—finally getting the consistency on the crust, and the inside it's still, well you said it best last time.

—Pillowy warmth.

—Pillowy warmth! You poet. Who have you brought?

—Maybe you know Gershwin?

—Mr. Mysterio, of course. A familiar face though I don't think we've ever spoken. Welcome.

—Satchel and Dunbar here, our poets.

—Writer, horseplayer, ex-teacher.

—Possibly soon-to-be lawyer.

—Talk about a mouthful. I've heard a thing or two about the legal profession but what is a horseplayer?

—I bet the ponies.

—My grandfather used to take me to Hawthorne for the, what is that race called—the Illinois Derby. He and his Polish cronies taught me to read the form, as they said, so interesting all of it—I never won, not once. Grampie called me his little bad luck charm.

—Maybe I've met your Grampie at the windows.

—*Couronnes* tonight. You all will be impressed. As well as a series of *Pain D'Epi*. Depending on your knowledge of the french language you might, or might not, pick up on the pun. Mona, Mona—I know you understand French quite well.

—Corona and wheat shafts?

—Gershwin, the maestro! *Tre bien*. Almost.

—Eclipsing the ear? Maybe, some sort of reference to blocking the sounds.

—You beautiful, beautiful, darling, joyful woman—yes! People criticize me for my esoteric themes—sorry, this is not Lincoln Park. Chicago will be run by intellectuals once again.

—To have a theme at all is daring.

—Gershwin, thank you. So the voices of others—chew them up, digest their fuel. On the cob, an ear of corn, right with *Pain D'Epi*, and this gorgeous circular bread a corona evident on the eclipse. We must come between what they say about us and our own sleeves. We must. Mr. Horseplayer, you must know this, am I correct?

—I am learning something new everyday.

—Never too old! Oh my Grampie, I miss him, I do. Alright, I will bring the bread—go join Mark and them by the fire.

Sienna and Mark had built the oven themselves out of salvaged materials: bricks, steel, rebar, metal, tin—I couldn't decipher it all but a bunch of random materials covered in a hardened clay mud and somehow holding the hot coals for the bread to cook. I went to look closer while Gershwin and Mark sat down by the fire. A few people stood up when they sat down and walked over to the oven, making sure I knew they knew all about it.

—S and M built this a year ago.

—They were just telling us about *restaurant plans*. It will be a bakery, right, but it will be seated like a restaurant.

—Marvelous butters and jams. Slices of *jamon* and lox.

—What an amazing couple.

—The thing I can't get over is why they built it here.

—I know. It lends something, though.

—What are you all talking about?

—The guy who built this house. What was his name? M was just telling us.

—Knut Nordlys.

—That's right. He hung himself. Was it in the kitchen?

—Yeah, and they buried him here.

—Or did he hang himself here and now he's buried in

the kitchen?

—When you talk to M, ask him and let us know.

—I think his remains are right below where S and M built the bread hearth. The building does have a distinctive Scandinavian touch, like those dragons carved into the trim along the roofline

—Playful political stuff. *Taking the city back,* as they say.

—S and M are like the most beautiful marriage of art and politics.

—And the bread?

—Divine!

Mona came over.

—Better than your welfare bread, right?

—I've got to step back a bit—it really gets hot.

—Look inside.

—Whoa. How do they create that circle of lava?

—Mark could explain best. It's like sub-thermal heating—there's a system of channels taking the fired wood down and bringing the lava up.

—The dead guy's down there?

—Reminds me of Mount Doom.

—I'm reading that to my kids right now! Currently on *Fellowship of the Ring.*

—God, my favorite Aunt read that to me when I was

young.

—What would you throw in the burning river at Mount Doom?

—I don't know, maybe a bra.

—An iron bra forged in the depths of Mordor. Fucking *Metal*.

—Torch the one bra which holds in all the boobs. Wait, no. I'd throw in a magazine cut-out of a person in the 60s who is burning a bra.

—Meta-metal.

—Destroy all those cultural and patriarchal reference points altogether, right? Let women just be and not have to worry about how what they do references back to previous liberation movements' agendas.

—I can't think of what would properly represent what I want to throw in.

—What is it?

—Voices. Advice. So many people, so many men, but either way just everyone telling everyone what to do with their lives. I feel like any advice people give is really just the advice they wished they heeded themselves.

—Kinda would suck to have to throw your ears into the lava.

—Take a blade and sever each ear above the molten air.

—Or your mind. It's like you need to ring out your

sponge, start fresh. Do you know Jodorowsky?

—One of those artists I hear people talk about, but I've never dove in.

—He taught me everything I know about the tarot, or at least his book did. That tarot book, really it's like the same energetic thrust of advice without any prescription or anxiety baked in. I love that guy. He does these healing ceremonies, like tarot readings mixed with the magical intentions of Catholic repentance. He reads your cards and you talk and he composes a ritual or a series of acts for you to do and heal. Can I give one to you?

—I'd love it.

—Okay. Let me think.

—So what's this deal with Jill again? What do you think she's up to?

—It sounds interesting right? Rituals, revolution—yes and yes. She's definitely sad, sweetie, you're cute to keep her in your thoughts. I'll be back.

—*I'll be back.*

—Even the Terminator? You do have a lot of voices circling around up there.

There were big laughs around the fire. Drunken laughters. The kind that make me wonder if they are laughing at whoever is not in earshot. But I walked over anyway. Two of the girls were holding court on Wicker

Park.

—I mean that place is a vampire! I walked down Milwaukee on a Thursday afternoon and by the time I got to Wood I had shaken seven suburban girls from my throat.

—I just can't understand what happened at Reckless Records.

—What happened?

—The clerks there would rather punch a nail through their feet than grab a record from the back.

—I asked one to make out with me and he didn't even respond.

—Oh, so you get it.

—You know what he did? Smirked. Just a smirk.

—It's like a nightmare from the 1990s.

—Okay but you did first ask him to find you Bon Iver's newest.

—Sorry that I fucking like Bon Iver!

—Who says *newest*?

I chimed in, thinking that I was matching the ethos with a real story as anecdote to the bad turn of the neighborhood.

—The night I met Dunbar, did you all meet Dunbar? Well, it was outside Reckless Records. He was living at the park kicking heroin and I couldn't decide if we had struck up a friendship or if he was on the hustle.

—What does he mean by *on the hustle?*

—He kept saying we should go see a specific movie he heard people at the park talking about. When he stopped by my apartment the next day to go catch *Training Day* at the Regal Theatre, he had the time all picked out, I had my roommate Jasper tell him I wasn't home. What was I afraid of?

No one said anything for a while.

—Yeah, well, back to Wicker Park—the place just isn't what it used to be.

—If you want to know what the neighborhood was, ask Dunbar.

—The junkie from your story, right?

—He's a poet. And he's right there.

Mark came out wheeling a butcher's block on casters stacked with loaves of bread. Gershwin was with him.

—Hi Gerswhin.

—Hey girls. How's it going? Steve—right?

—It's David. You can call me Dave.

—Where are you headed after this, Gersh?

—I'm trying to talk Satchel into hitting up a noise show at The Coat Factory.

— You all are keeping it real.

—I know, right? They're like throwbacks.

—We're more Brick Garden types.

—Is that the commune of musicians over on North Avenue?

—I wouldn't call it that.

—I had a student last year who would go there, her name was Grace. And at that time a horse named Grace Hall was running. I would bet that runner every time.

—Did she win?

—Why do you like horse racing?

—She won a lot at first but then lost like eight races in a row, ended up costing me some money.

—My name is Sylmar—you can bet on that.

—Really?

—That's where my parents lived when they had me but they had to move from LA because they couldn't afford it.

—The Princess of Sylmar, easy enough?

—What's that supposed to mean?

—There's a filly named Princess of Sylmar.

—Wow Satch you have got it bad! What a magician.

—Only if she wins, otherwise just a fool. I had a dream a couple weeks ago, listen to this, it wasn't a typical dream. It was just a song I woke up with in my head.

—Yeah and?

—*Waking up in a basement in Moreno. Wondering if there's someplace I gotta go. Brushed my teeth and played boogie woogie on piano. Realized today that I just might be free.*

Sienna entered.

—I didn't know this would be that kind of campfire—but phenomenal, there's always a first—my friends, your bread.

—No, but there was a horse named Moreno and he just won last week. I'll keep betting him.

—First, eat the *Couronnes* and *Pain D'Epi*.

—The glow of being in earshot.

—Eclipsing the voices.

—So many nuances to translation and yes and yes and please feast and be full towards your *you*. That is the goal my, campfire singers—your you.

—But honestly, every time I'm in Wicker Park all I see is Suburbanites and hipsters.

—You need to start exploring the city's gray areas, man.

—Sounds like the name of a shitty band that plays insipid songs.

—I bet Satch is wondering if there's a horse named Gray Areas.

Big laughs. I sat there smiling my best *fuck you* smile. Everybody fell back to talking with their immediate neighbors. Gerswhin had sat down next to me.

—This bread has a great crust.

—Okay. Maybe I'm too cynical?

—Dude, it's bread, S and M made it—that's sincere. Eat it and love it.

—You mean Sienna and Mark.

—What's your deal?

—I'm just worn thin with it all. And this Coup de Brew...

—First, noise. Then, we'll see if we stop by. Dunbar's coming with us. He was inside on their couch preparing to hit it, and I said *hold up hold up, we're hitting The Coat Factory*. He looked at me, shivered and said *brrrrrr*.

—There's Mona. The night would end without her.

—Hey, you coming to The Coat Factory with us?

—Satchel! You ready for your instructions?

—I've got Samwise and Gandolf at my side.

—It took me a minute to rustle through their apartment but I found it. Come here.

I got up and walked towards her and she led me back towards the hearth where we last talked.

—Take this. I'm so, so pleased. They had a real sponge in their bathroom—like from-the-sea real.

—That's got to be expensive.

—All the better for this ceremony if it is. I just tore off a hunk. Feel it. Hard, right? Put it in your bag.

131

—Not much room in there.

—Make room. Toss shit out, you must follow every instruction for this to work. The next time you hear anything resembling advice, you need to take this out and soak up whatever liquid is nearby in the same room as the words you hear. Are you ready for this?

—Yes.

—Then you need to squeeze every last liquid once on the head of the voice that you hear.

—I'll get punched in the face!

—Exactly. Advice givers are punch throwers. You need to put down your shields and take the hit. Then use the sponge to soak up the spilt blood. Put it back in your bag. Travel with it. Like the wind carrying the seeds of a sacred tree, you must take it somewhere else. And dig a hole in the earth to plant it.

—Okay, and then I'll be healed.

—No. Now you have your item to throw into the hellfire of Mount Doom.

—What?

—Your blood-stained messenger bag.

—This? Why this? I've carried it around this city for a decade.

—Once the sponge is planted, you must throw your bag into the first fire you see.

—You are one wicked Dungeon Master.

—Terrence is gonna love hearing about this. Do you accept the journey as it has been told to you?

—Can I bring along your bra for good measure?

—I'm not wearing one.

—Oh. Then a kiss.

As Mona leaned in and kissed me on the cheek, I turned my lips to meet hers. She pushed her body into mine and I ran my hand through her wild red curls, lit from head to toe as a fire traveled from my mouth through my lungs down my spine and expanded across every inch of my body. My hand lingered on her hip as she pulled away. I opened my eyes to see her golden irises and her smile.

—Take this, Satchel.

—Are you coming with me?

—Jill, you know, she's struggling. I'm going to go find her. Whatever this event is that she told me about, it could be worthwhile knowing about.

—Maybe I'll see you there.

—That kiss was just part of the spell. I needed you to feel unbridled.

—There's a horse named Unbridled's Note running at Churchill next week in a race before the Kentucky Derby.

—You are the horse's name you need to hear. Bye.

Mona turned away to go as Dunbar walked up, slouched and shuffling his feet. I stuffed the sponge into my messenger bag.

—Dunbar, come on with it, we're out!

—On it, man. Let me just find my bike.

CHAPTER EIGHTEEN

There was no bike rack nearby The Coat Factory so we each stopped separately and found a lamp post or parking meter to lock up on. The mood of our little group shifted, a little more serious as if we were preparing entry into a different ring of influence. The night-after-night reinitiation into the inner neighborhood.

It was dark. Candlelit. Everyone at the bar was intent on drinking their drink. In conversation. In gloom. If you wanted to know the moods, these were the moody. I knew not to ask who was playing. I knew not to think about what I wanted to drink. I knew not to laugh and joke. I knew not to be loud. I knew not to be soft. I knew not to be anything but to be being and look forward to the having been.

I knew all this, but I smiled, wondering who in the room would give me advice. I bought whiskeys for the three of us but made the bartender mad when I forgot to say which.

—Let's make it Wild Turkey. One for you, too. And four PBRs.

I passed the shots to Gershwin and Dunbar and raised mine to cheers, which they reluctantly joined.

—Let's get the bartenders drunk and the band drunker

and when we pass out in the snow, let our guardian's prayers be answered.

—I think Razor is sober, Satch.

—The band is straight edge. A little bit too on the nose if you ask me.

—Satch and 'Shwin, what about this garden tonight? Let's hit it up.

—You don't want to stay here too long?

—Duration of stay is the least of my concerns. Just so long as we reach that peak—are they firing away in there yet?

We looked to the back room, our eyes trying to pull sound for our ears' answer. Behind the door to the back room, a rustic warmth built in the air.

—Sounds like maybe some rustling of beginnings.

—These Razors don't cut through the skin for like twenty minutes. At first you think the blade was there to scratch an itch and then they slice ya open. As long as I'm here for that, then after is after. This garden thing is over on Rockwell north of Milwaukee. Bunch of freaks will be doing their thing planting seeds and seedlings—kind of a mind maze gang.

—Shit, that's real close to Coup de Brew.

—You all heading in? I've gotta see the man about a horse.

Gershwin and I had found a spot standing along a wall with a ledge for drinks. The noise began slowly, quietly. We stared at it, wondering how it would rise, what shape it would take, and out of the corner of our eyes came Dunbar waddling over to find us. His toes dipped upon the floor as if the noise materialized an obstacle course and his chin nodded along irrhythmically as if heavier now and he needed to reacquaint his muscles and bones with the distribution of mass throughout his body. The two guitars on stage played no guitar, but the strings were buttons for the musicians' distortion which wobbled and grew like a muddy blob dripping up from the earth. They punched out a migratory high pitch and Dunbar's chin dropped to his waist, as if his face was wanting to disappear through the hardwoods. Someone behind Dunbar reacted, reaching between his arms to brace and soothe him, then rolling their forearms up his torso to his chest and Dunbar smiled, soothed. No one spoke. The point of being there was not to talk. Like ears were not enough, our entire bodies had to listen.

Dunbar waddled further and positioned against the wall. As the noise grew tentacles, grew wet fur and spastic parasites, more and more errors began to occur, ideas or instances of approach that were soon erased by a return to the ground the musicians had lifted from the sky. The goofiest eyes-closed grin spread across Dunbar's face, wider with each spasm of noise-infected emotion, I would say joy but it seemed more like any and every emotional phenomenon worked viscerally through his endocrine system. His head began to bob and weave and his eyes splashed open. Then I saw that everyone around us was lost in their own bodies, exploring perilous channels of consciousness and excavating pituitary crannies and penalized nooks for some state of awareness which is offered in this life though not easily accessed.

The guy next to me looked about my age and as the noise began to rise up, his eyes opened and his arms lifted to hit his DMT. He sensed me and did not turn in my direction but his hands floated in front of my face offering the glass pipe. Everyone in the room was somewhere else and I could join them for an eternal thirty minutes. Like a beer coasting down the bar, I took his hand and gilded it back in front of his face. No muscle moved and no motion of his head besides his lips.

—Guess this scene's not for you.

Then he put the lighter beneath the glass and ripped. I drifted out of the crowd, back towards the bar to order another beer. That wasn't technically advice. Gershwin soon came looking for me.

—How are the horses?

—Good. Or some good, some not.

—A man and his gambles. Any dream winners since Geology?

—San Giacomo.

—Right.

—Shared Belief most recently, Magician before that. It is the damnedest thing—makes me believe in a god.

—How so?

—Or at least that we have access to the future, but if there is some sort of way for these things to come to me from the future, then there must be a system in place, a logic, and an overseeing presence organizing the chaos.

—Maybe your future you is sending back winners. So that you can continue writing.

—I like that. That's really nice.

—Might cost you your savings to find out but what the hell, right?

—I hear you, but it feels like everything is on the line with this decision.

—What's at stake?

—Everything or nothing. That's the essence of spiritual decisions.

—No, that's the essence of religion and that's why religious fuckers are so dogmatic, don't be dogmatic. I don't need to know whether there is something or nothing at stake, it shouldn't matter, I should still exist in the same way.

—But existence is more than inertia, you have volition, will, you can create, push forth, piss off. You can transform.

—Transform?

—Like a butterfly. There's no other way.

—Death takes care of that.

—You are right, but maybe life is where the colors of your wings are born.

—It's not a competition to have the brightest wings.

—I think all life is at work expressing itself and humans are accelerants on the earth. Making connections and organizing intelligences. We are transformers.

—*More than meets the eye.*

—So, what do you have to lose?

—Michelle. I don't know how long she can put up with me stumbling around in the clouds like this.

—You've always been like this, right? She's with you, trust me.

—Oh that's right, she wanted me to tell you *hi*.

—You two are lucky.

—I want to be successful at what I do. It really sucks writing books that no one reads.

—Yeah, I think that's why so many step aside from art.

We wonder if we can do it, we try, and then if we don't get the reception we expected, we bail.

—I want to do right by my kids.

—As long as you love them, how could you go wrong?

—I also want to figure life out, my life, how to get all the good stuff out of me and how to bring all the good stuff of the world in.

—When we made that album in college, you know, we were new to the city, tapped into each other, surrounded by all this energy. But when I think back about it, for me at least, it was an inner thing. That first part of what you said —I felt like I was ringing out a bell that had always been inside. So, is being a lawyer that for you?

—I'm feeling drunk, man. It's hard to hear.

—Life's easier when you are drunk.

—No, it's easier when you're high.

—I was so high when we made that album in college.

—Let's fire up as we ride out of here.

—Cool if we swing by the brewery?

—I give you a hard time, but whatever you do, now I'm behind you. Let's get the fuck out of here.

—I thought that was pretty good shit.

—What about Dunbar?

—He's shining his bell.

—My man has got a full-fledged gong in there.

CHAPTER NINETEEN

The tip of the lake winds darted down Fullerton, making it difficult to light the joint. Gershwin didn't realize I was slow to get going and shot off. I legged up and began a slow pedal. West Fullerton Street felt river-wide. Looking a block up I saw Allen pushing a stroller through the intersection. I shouted his name but he stared straight ahead, lost in the neighborhood where he'd made a reputation as a musician, now saddled with sleepless, midnight baby walks. I wondered if Wayne was at the Whirlaway, maybe Allen was going to meet him there. Then I remembered that Wayne had moved home to LA.

My pedaling slowed down and before I knew it Gershwin had already turned on Milwaukee. In the door of the Two-Way Lounge I saw Pookie laughing, drunkenly yelling back and forth with a pit bull-walking gutter punk. Two CPD SUVs pulled up to the 7-Eleven in a hurry, but the cops only meandered out, no action, just hungry and flaunting guns.

From Fullerton down on Milwaukee it was bar after bar, broken up only by a mechanic and a pawn shop—the fabric of the great American city now threadbare and patched with nylon. I saw the irony of this critique being made by someone about to walk into the brewery that signaled the sea change, and it made me mad. I didn't hang out with guys like Gershwin to hit up places like this.

—Satchel!

I slowed down and looked back. There was Dunbar, hustling along, smiling huge.

—We hitting the brewery? Don't forget about the garden, man!

Coup de Brew looked closed, so we followed Gershwin into the alley and chained our bikes on a couple dumpsters. Gershwin pounded on the back door, and it took a bit before the door swung open, and a man named Camarillo smiled.

—Hey hey! Amigos!

—What's up Camarillo?

— *Trés borrachos*. You stink.

—Hard work riding around these streets.

—*Pinché* bicycle bullshit. Close the door, don't let *jefe* hear you—he's not happy tonight.

—What happened?

—They were filming a show and this guy, *puto's* name was Guy I think, he didn't come, so *jefe's* pissed. Hey, send back a tequila for the *muchachos*, alright?

Mick, the owner, was behind the bar talking with two guys—Fred and Chris, Michelle's friends from high school. I remembered Michelle had told me they recently bought neighboring graystones in Logan Square with the ungodly sum they made from selling their mobile app. Fucking Fred and Chris, and other than them and Mick that was it besides the kitchen staff, singing out and laughing as their tapedeck rattled through songs from home.

—Well, at least they read the sign: *Hippies use the back entrance.*

—Assholes, this is my place. Gershwin's a friend.

—Wait, that's Satchel. We go all the way to goddamn Evanton to see the man while he's been hiding in our neighborhood.

—Buddy? We left your apartment like thirty minutes ago.

—Couldn't make it tonight, guys. How was it?

—Digging your man-bag, Satchel.

I hung my bag on the back of the bar seat next to them and took the next seat over. Dunbar perched suspiciously to my left. Leaning over the bar, Gershwin set up to get his face time with Mick as he polished the brass taps.

—Michelle is always more fun when you're not around. Don't worry, buddy.

—It looks like tonight's the night we hang no matter

which way you cut it.

—Don't sound so happy to see us.

—Hey, Mick. Not too late I hope.

—Glad you made it Gershwin.

—Mind pouring a round of tequilas?

—Now that's the way to make it nice. We'll forgive Satchel for not showing up.

—To his own house.

—Fellas, I'm Gershwin. We've met a couple times.

—We know you, buddy. Mick's always going on about how you could bring in good business.

—I guess there are people in this neighborhood that go wherever Rey Mysterio goes.

—Not sure about all that.

—Fred and Chris bought in a couple weeks ago, Gershwin, we've been talking about how to grow this place.

—Mick, he's the one who might open up the brewery in Pilsen?

—That's a ways off. Six tequilas for now. Herradura sound alright?

—If it's anything like your last one, we'll be taking the brewery across the country.

—How about a few more for Camarillo and the kitchen crew. I can buy.

—They almost done back there? I think Patrón is their weapon of choice.

—Sorry I didn't make it here on time for the film crews, Mick.

—We needed you, baby, a whole lot of suburbanites up in here tonight. We're going to look dorky as fuck. They just grabbed B-roll.

—B-roll, I think that's what your friend is on.

—Dunbar, you alright?

—Just sitting here waiting for the horseshoe.

—Fucking weirdo.

—His Spanish as good as yours, Gersh? I could use a go-between making sure they aren't stealing as much as I think they are.

—I don't know Spanish. Is that what *herradura* means?

—To business, *mi amigos*.

—Mick, what about adding a tequila tasting menu to the Pilsen location?

—To luck.

Saying this I looked at Gershwin, half connecting back to our conversations and half showing him how much anger I was swallowing to be there on this night with these people. He winked and clinked our shot glasses.

—That's smooth, bartender—*muchas gracias*.

—Glad you two stopped by on your way home. So you

were up at this guy's house before this?

—Satchel's wife was our good friend growing up.

—Fred and her, everyone thought they would get married.

—Who marries their high school girlfriend?

—The way you two were talking tonight—like old times.

—Sorry Satch, don't listen to him. Michelle seems like she's doing good—your kids are hilarious.

—I'm sure you hear it from her, but your place, bro, it doesn't cut it. Michelle has class, you gotta step it up.

The tequila hit me like you want tequila to hit you. I felt bulletproof.

—Your gang doing alright? Nathan was a sad deal. Let's do another for Nathan. Mick, I'm buying this one.

—Put your money away.

—We shed some tears tonight. A lot to be sad about.

—To Nathan. The only one of Michelle's friends who liked me.

—To Nathan.

—What's that shit, Satch? How's this for not liking you—we came up to your house tonight to see if you want to get in with us on our next project.

—Fred, we were just saying we might want to scrap that.

—We didn't see the whole picture yet, Chris. Here's the pitch: low six figures to start but really no ceiling to how much this can turn into for you, Satchel.

—Now this is surprising.

—We need someone who knows this city, who knows cities and artists.

—Yeah and who can write. We need the language to be right on this one. Scope was all collecting data and it was right for its time, but data combined with the right appeal is what has the most traction these days.

—Scope is the app you all sold? Gershwin, it aggregated the average age of each storefront's customers. Neat, right?

—It was much more than an app.

—You can come up with your own title, we don't care, maybe Lead Field Scout, something like that, but we'd have you traveling to different cities and getting a sense for the trends, the language they are using, collecting it, reporting back. We'd want you to hire a team, be their leader.

—I wouldn't even call it work. Everyone would get a phone with trackers that feed back relevant data, you'd be taking pictures, doing internal reports, and we'd team up to sift through it all and find the golden nuggets.

—There's dozens of industries who would pay for this.

—Pay for what?

—First it's an app—you and your team would have the beta version, but it's a social way to interact with the city so that you know who's been where, and where the people you are interested in are going. But it collects data, too, so everyone who uses it, a becomes a nerve-ending tuned into a city's scene.

—We project millions of users between the ages of 16 and 27,

—City Bod is the working title.

—How about Dad Bod?

—That's just it, Satch—you're a dad, we want to help you out.

—Sounds interesting, but we didn't come here for me. Gershwin and Mick are cooking up something.

—I don't want to speak for him, but I think they're sorting all that out now.

Mick and Gershwin were huddled over a bar napkin. Dunbar had taken the tequilas to the kitchen and hadn't returned. Their radio now dialed between two neighboring stations so the music of each blurred together, one song occasionally coming through a little clearer, buried in the static hissing. I heard Camarillo laughing about this *pinche loco güero.*

—So this is a job offer? Like, I'd start tomorrow?

—Whoa, horsey, not tomorrow—we'll be sleeping this

one off tomorrow—but yeah, we could meet up next week and sign off on it all.

—Did you tell Michelle?

—Of course. She was, well, she was excited.

—Excited? Fuck. She looked like a pair of anvils had been lifted off both her shoulders.

—Yeah well she thought you'd be perfect for City Bod, and she said you'd been considering law school and all that.

—Fred, when you say City Bod, it's not doing it for me.

—What about Cityman?

—I think we need to ditch the word city.

—What was it the consultant came up with?

—Orb?

—Orb.

—He's running in the Derby.

—What?

—There's a Kentucky Derby horse named Orb. It's next week.

—You think it's copyrighted or something?

—No I think I'm gonna bet him.

—What's this you're pouring, Mick?

—Sorry to interrupt all your horseshit. One more beer and one more cheers. Gershwin is coming onboard.

—I'll be in the kitchen to start.

—Wherever you see fit, Gersh—we just want you on our team.

—I think we settled on the name for our new project.

—Please tell me it's not City Bod.

—Orb.

—Wait, wait, wait. I was just being polite. I'm not seriously thinking about working for you two.

—You're kidding.

—He's kidding.

—Satchel's got a lot on his mind—give him some time to think it over.

—Rey Mysterio's right—not the right time of day for making decisions. Go home, talk with Michelle, look at your kids, and let us know.

—No, I don't need to think it over. That tequila makes me as clear-headed as I'd ever want to be.

—I just tapped this fresh tonight. It's a hoppy hefeweizen named After the Gold Rush. My favorite Neil Young album.

—Fred, isn't that what you and Michelle used to put on in your bedroom?

—What the fuck did you say?

—Don't get your panties in a bunch, Satchman.

—Gershwin, tell this guy to make nice or I can pour him a growler to go.

—Your lady is cool, man. You got lucky.

—Yeah, but she didn't.

—I knew I hated you two the first time I met you. Michelle feels the same, that's why you never see her.

—We never see her because she's too busy working and taking care of your kids, you fucking deadbeat.

—I poured you a beer, either drink it and stop talking shit or leave. Gershwin isn't this your professor friend?

—If Satchel was your teacher, you're already fucked.

—You two are fucking dickholes.

—No, we're dick holes who like fucking.

Dunbar came wondering in from the kitchen where Starship's "We built This City" played and Camarillo was belting out his best version as the crew clanged pots and pans.

—Chicago—come for the hoes, stay for the bros. Who are these people anyway, Gershy?

—What did you do to my kitchen staff?

—It's natural, don't worry.

—Finish 'em up. Night's over.

—I wouldnt be your fucking lead spy for any amount of money.

—Alright, Satchel, enough man, really.

But I wasn't through.

—You come following the crowd into the neighborhood,

buying into this unimaginative cog of capitalism.You two used to talk shit on people who lived here. We'd see your pathetic team of friends at some bullfuck place in Lincoln Park Michelle would drag me to so she could be nice and pretend like she hasn't forgotten the people she escaped from. Now you live here because that's all you can do in this life. Follow. You don't like me, I don't like you, so don't give me this six-figure job bullshit. Stay the fuck out of our life.

—Some life you got buddy. Very impressive. It will be so hard to stay away.

—Listen, I'm ready to kick the shit out of you two. And the fucking craft beerman—fuck him.

—Get the fuck out of my bar.

—Take a swing.

—My insurance rate will go up if I kick your ass in my bar.

—Listen, Satchel's drunk. He'll calm down—we've been drinking a few tonight.

—You're right. Poor guy. He's out of work, collecting unemployment, while his wife is wishing she'd never met him. Get a job, you bozo.

That sounded like advice to me. I reached down and grabbed the sponge from my messenger bag.

—The fuckign loser is grabbing some drugs.

I lifted the beer Mick had poured and stuffed the sponge in, soaking up half the pint.

—This is such a weird night. Let's go, Chris.

Standing up on the rung of my barstool, I squeezed most of the beer over Fred, then rung out the rest on Chris.

—Fuck you!

—Get out of here, Satch. Go.

Gershwin pulled me out of my chair and pushed me towards the door as I was yelling.

—Those two are coming with me.

Fred and Chris jumped out of their stools but Gershwin held them back.

—Dunbar, take Satchel out front and smoke a cigarette

—I don't smoke!

—Put a piece of Nicorette in his mouth and close it. I will be right behind you.

I did want a cigarette. I leaned against a wall and looked at the streetlamps shielding the black sky, never a star, the Blue Line screeching past under the pseudoephedrine hands of the conductor, two women laughing together in friendship on the other side of the street. Dunbar mumbling to me things I wouldn't remember, a few cars passing, Banda music and a big grin across the driver's face, or was it utter seriousness.

Then Gershwin came through the alley rolling our bikes.

Fred and Chris behind him.

—Let's go. Where's this garden, Dunbar? Just get the fuck out of here.

—Okay.

—You alright?

—Let's not go too fast.

—Cool.

I wobbled forward but felt a kick on my tire, sending me flying to the curb.

—Fuck you, you fucking loser.

I knew my face was wet but I was too numb to taste that it was blood. It had to hurt, and my ribs and wrist were sore, but it felt good, too. Gershwin helped me up, and I smiled. I felt the fire.

—Fuck them. You okay?

—How do I look?

—Like someone dropped an anvil on your face.

I took out the sponge, which I shoved in my pocket. I rung it out one more time and patted down my face, mopping up the blood. Then I shoved it into my bag.

I played up my stumble and pathetic state, wobbling over to Fred and Chris and I looked at them, focusing the best I could. I had to hurt them.

—Looks like that cut across your face might scar. Michelle won't be able to forget who was right.

—I might be a sad sack of shit, but you are a corporate boardroom cumrag.

I tackled them both with one throw of my body, flailing my arms and elbows, screaming.

—You sucked the soul out of Chicago!

I spit all over them like one intense angsty purge of everything that began to ball up angrily inside since I was a teenager. I got up and grabbed my bike before they could snag my legs, lifting it over my head—I can still see my shadow cast over their bodies by the streetlights—and slammed it on them, hearing something crack.

Then again I was on the ground. Dunbar had pushed me.

—You should know better. Don't let men like this into your mind, Satch.

—Fuck you, Satchel! You broke Chris' arm!

—My arm's fine!

—The bone, man, I can see the bone out of your skin.

—What the fuck!

—Listen you faggot, I see your fucking future. No law school. No books. Stooping over at the horse track looking for winning tickets in the trash. Where will Michelle and your kids be then? Where, you selfish cunt, where?!

I hollered and fake nunchucked his face as Dunbar hustled my bike to my side.

—Hop on. Let's go plant some veggies.

Chapter Twenty

We were off without far to go. My head throbbed and my thoughts shrieked. These men in my head. They never liked the looks of me. I had to hurt them, I had to try—I didn't know why I had waited so long to break through the surface and find the bone. The voices began compulsively backfiring, and a swarm of furious sound bites, images and mania spewed forth. Now the marrow could be known.

My father stared through me asking *A writer—what about making a living for your family?* My uncle mocked my choice of teaching. *There's no money in teaching—your family didn't make sacrifices for you to become a teacher.* My brother and brother-in-laws all flashed appearances saying what they had to say about a guy like me, who was no man, just a boy they could never understand. The voices scoffed at my life, critiqued and ridiculed me with sneers. *You gotta be kidding me about this horse racing bullshit. Just buck up, fade your emotions and do what you have to do. Do what you have to do!* my father-in-law dressed in drill-sergeant drag screamed in my face, *I do not respect a husband, a father who doesn't make money!*

They studied me but never could get a glimpse of the vision I strained to bring to life. They shook their head at my childishness, *what sacrifices have you made, Satchel? You'll understand one day, Satch,* they all said, patronizing me, emasculating me, infantilizing me. *One day you'll see.* And they were right, I had seen what they warned me I would see, and in the face of it I had almost reversed course.

We shot down Rockwell to Lyndale. Dunbar's friends' garden was across the street from a neighborhood school. Piles of bikes stacked and locked on every fence up and down the block—if a neighbor looked out their window, they would feel besieged. We locked our bikes halfway down the street in an open spot where someone must have just left, and I looked across the street to see it was Goethe Elementary.

I unbuttoned my shirt and used my undershirt to wipe the blood from my eyes and nose. I stared ahead to see if I could focus. Gershwin put his arm around my shoulders.

—Sorry about that, man. I'm sorry.

—So you took the job.

—I just can't pass on this.

—As soon as you trust yourself, you will know how to live. If not, you'll sit forever, gluing things together, cooking up a stew from other's scraps, blowing on a miserable fire made from your heap of dying ash.

—That might be the most poetic thing you've said all

night.

—Just make sure you can live with yourself when you turn thirty-five.

—Twenty-year-old me would be pissed but I bet thirty-five-year-old me will be able to stomach it.

We stood staring at a vacant lot, a nascent garden that over the summer months would grow flush with corn and tomato, fruit trees and flowering bushes. An abandoned building on one side and a six-flat apartment rental on the other. Upon arrival, I was not ready to begin sobering— but I embraced this event if nothing else as an anecdote to Coup de Brew. There was little here to excite—no art, no alcohol, no music, chatter reserved to needing to maneuver around each other—just the night and the earth and the humans who go between the two.

—Gershwin, I think he wants you for your cachet.

—And I want him for his money.

—Right.

—You two coming in or going to keep unwinding the fibonacci sequence until you realize the center's rule?

—Dunbar, you never fail to illuminate.

—He's all light with no need to be seen.

—Lead us onward.

There was an entrance, and once through I could see dozens of people wandering the rows of sprouts and seedlings. Still a high likelihood of frost throughout the month of May, I felt this ritual was as much a symbol of optimism as it was a fool's gamble. If the first plantings survived, there would be an early bounty of asparagus, garlic scapes, onions, fennel, and lettuce. If temperatures dropped, the gardeners would have to start over again.

—What's next with you and your bloody sponge?

—That's right. Mona said I need to dig a hole and plant it.

—I'll dig for you, my man. That sucked back there, but maybe, you know, it was time for you to say fuck you to some things.

—I hope Michelle understands.

—Just pray what grows from this will lift you with it. Actions, man. Actions are the way we communicate with fate. The cosmos struggles to read our minds but when we act, it knows.

I took a knee where Gershwin had dug, pulled the bloody sea sponge out and placed it at the bottom of the hole. My hands, my bag, my blood, and my mind recalled how the midwest is the descendant of a long, shallow, inland sea that's been gone for more than 60 million years. I'd seen fossils of sponges on hikes Michelle and I had taken in various parts of Illinois and Wisconsin, and as I brushed the dirt back into the hole, I wondered if other lawyers had taken similar roads.

When we got to the center of the lot, we found a small square fence which we circled until realizing that to enter, we had to crawl underneath. There was a spot which generations of rabbits must have created. As if the rabbits knew there was something worthwhile on the other side and chewed at the wood slats and dug away at the dirt to create a passage. Gershwin and Dunbar waved off the task and kept walking, but I got on my knees, then fell to my belly to slide and pull my way through the hole.

An obelisk-like sculpture stood tall at the center of the fenced-off plot which was no bigger than twelve-by-twelve feet. Each side presented a mercury glass mirror, far older than the ones I had been mesmerized by in barrooms across the city. I inspected each pane until I found the one lit by the full moon, which had crossed its apex and now filled much of the top portion. I could faintly see my reflection through the mottled glass, clouded by tarnished blotches and streaks. Layered beneath the stormy discolorations, portions of the mirror sparkled in the moonlight, which I watched slide so slowly next to my face.

Instead of a pyramid atop the tower, there was a bronze pinecone. I reached up and touched it, leaving a residue of oil on my fingertips that smelled of fleshy innards. I felt compelled to do the three signs of the cross on my forehead, my lips, and my heart, as I had done so many times at St. Francis in grade school, but then I carried it downwards adding my solar plexus, my stomach, and the bottom of my spine. Instead of the heaviness this ritual had always laid upon me in church, doing it then made me lift—a levity I recalled feeling when young but it had been so long. How serious I had been—how stricken with seriousness—how necessary the perception of light and the acceptance of sleep. If only to let in dreams, those murkiest of images which momentarily sneak across the divide like a bolt of lightning momentarily splayed and pinned. Out from a center and according to a sequence we must trust, still the dream's intention is to cause us to swerve.

Without pretense I reached to repeat the signs of the cross on my reflection, beginning at the base of my spine and working up. I added a seventh sign of the cross, and as I pushed my thumb upon the mirrored top of my balding head, I fell within.

I took a left and headed to the river.

Chapter Twenty One

At Cortland I crossed the bridge, stopped above the river and watched a junker barge, and then a trash heap float along the dark waters.

Ahead I saw the giant hangar door was rolled open at A. Finkl & Sons Steel Plant. I slowed down to watch the giant blast furnaces smelting the liquid steel. The glow of the molten lava warmed my eyes. There was more activity inside the foundry than I had ever seen before. The darting bodies and shadows of bats or raccoons eclipsing the red glow.

I leaned against a parking meter and looked around past the first building of A. Finkl & Sons to see the entire campus extending on each side of Cortland. Like rhizomes, each cavernous building grew off the next and I became overwhelmed to consider the extent of steel manufacturing taking place in our American night. What would the body do with all this—how could it be digested?

Prunella Ashton, my old friend, walked out through the hangar door. Once upon a time we worked together at a deli in Bucktown, and at that time, the Humboldt Park apartment she shared with Abraham was the center of our artist scene. They fed the group, hosted pot lucks, and tended to the vision—we were artists, we would be bound to each other and shape a world separate from capitalism's hold on the imagination. Ash, as we called her, and Abe were younger than me by less than a decade. They were both sculptors who had met at the School of the Art Institute of Chicago but dropped out at the end of the first year, deciding to work at the deli and deepen their foundry work through befriending ironworkers at the bar where the union members drank. They took all of us out to Burning Man several years in a row—our group having grown to include many from the steel mills, the neighboring shops, the bartenders—leading our creations.

Standing at 5 feet 3 inches in platform boots, Ash waved to me and scrunched up her side lip in her signature grin.

—Ash!

—Hey man.

I kept my eyes open leaning in for a hug, seeing behind her what had been hidden to me before: a dozen or so of her gang, a few I recognized, working fiercely either rolling in giant carts of metal scraps or handing objects up to Abe who stood on a platform above, throwing the pieces into a giant cauldron, cooking off the impurities.

—We're dislodging tonight.

—You all good? Still doing it?

—Making it.

That's what she always said. Making it, as in getting by but also as in creating, doing.

I tried to be gregarious, but the wit and zing had left me, and I remembered that my mania never fed Ash's energy.

—It's been too long.

—Yeah. You know. I just stepped out for a breath, but we're hauling ass in there. Did you ever do one of these with us? When the time comes, you'll remember what to do.

—I'm in.

The only light source in the cavernous building was the molten metal's bright glow from the giant cauldron. It took a bit for my eyes to adjust, and even then I didn't understand how the figures could move so rapidly in and out of the shadows. Like a rat king reanimated, they each shot away from the cauldron at the center but only as far as their tails would allow, tied to this task at hand. They wore thick dank pants, white shirts stained and shadowed gray over their ashen and greasy skin, combat boots, rags like bandanas around their heads or wrists or necks. I nodded at the familiar faces, but my presence was unwarranted and no one needed to engage with me.

I wandered around trying to make sense of what

they were up to. Cart upon cart of miscellaneous scrap metal—the bare frame of an old Bowflex machine, bikes, truck gates, newspaper dispensers, hub caps, fenders, shredded train cars, kitchen appliances, stoves, poles, street signs—piled up near the giant drum. They were taking turns handing items to Abe or heaving the lighter ones up themselves, as Abe stirred the molten pot.

Others had been busy that night welding various objects into monstrous bikes, unconforming gnarly hulks as tall as the forge drum, much more ornate than we ever accomplished at Burning Man. They pedaled chaotically and swerved to miss each other, chugging beers and throwing the empty cans into the lava.

I didn't have anything to say. Occasionally the cauldron tipped and poured into the molds, and I wondered what weights they forged. I found a warm Stag Beer on the ground and opened it.

Ash carried a ladder over her head towards the drum. She leaned it against the balcony, and that's when I noticed Jill walking next to her. I looked for Mona in the nest of shadows. Nowhere to be seen, but I felt again the heat of her kiss spread throughout my body, burning away so many postures.

Abe descended and Ash climbed to the top. Then, Jill and my old friend Lottie began handing her the welded creations which Ash lifted and let go into the cauldron. Her small frame mightily heaving the heavy scrap metal, and when the last monstrous bike was brought to her, all had gathered near to watch Ash lift this giant deformity and toss it over the lip of the drum. Immediately everyone went berserk and the rat king was no longer as their tails broke free. All the figures running in every direction, scurrying and colliding, yelling maniacally.

Ash was right. Everything came back to me.

I began a mad sprint to the cauldron, lifting my messenger bag from over my head, but as I brought my arm back to throw it in, a body rammed into me and knocked me on the ground, sending the leather bag sliding across the cement floor. The adrenaline overpowered the wind being knocked out of me and I pushed myself up from the ground. I saw an arm grab the bag and began twirling it overhead as they ran in figure eights laughing. I looked up and saw Ash swinging her arms and eyes around like a conductor of the frenzy, tilting the drum to pour the molten mixture into the molds. Far into the building, the molds were set to cool on a conveyor belt that extended for miles into the deep throat of the cavern. They were making new forms for us to swallow.

I picked a half-drunk beer up off the floor and swallowed the last sips of Stag, crushed the can with my foot and hurled it at the vat. As I turned to leave, I saw Jill carrying a bar stool over her head, roaring and approaching the cauldron. She tried to heave it over the edge but before falling in, the seat burst into flames and it tipped back, falling on top of her and knocking her to the ground.

I hustled to her, kicking the stool away, and grabbed her hands to bring her back to her feet. She was unhinged and though I could see burns across her arms, she leapt towards the stool as it rolled away, still in flames, lifted it by the legs, and spun towards the caldron with a final bounce as she swung the stool ablaze up high above and down into the cauldron. Jill puffed out her chest and let out a sound so wild it rang out deep within my bones, setting my marrow abuzz.

After that it was like I was watching myself move through the cavern, unconscious of what I was doing but running, screaming, bouncing off the others in the disentangled fury of humans untethered. My bag hung around the neck of another and I saw myself tackle him and yank it free, breaking the strap in half. Immediately I took off running, hollering at the fire, at the humans, at the night, at my life, at the bag and the unfinished task Mona had set off inside me, and I watched it fly at first in darkness through the air, then momentarily lit up above the caldron as it set to fire before landing in the lava.

I burst, momentarily unbound, filling every infinite inch of the room and beyond. In that instant I knew every street every alley every staircase and fire escape every room of every apartment every terrace and park subway tunnel and bus line. Atop every building all at once I had a vision of a hurtling meteorite colliding with Chicago followed by a massive wind and then nothing remained but that alien iron rock atop the earth. I knew I was this. I knew this was here to stay.

Then I settled back behind my eyes, felt sweat and grime across my body, Jill's blood and my own. It was as if I had spent a lifetime hovering above my body but never fully dropping in as I settled down into every cell, fully radiant and knowing how good the lake waters would feel and that I had the strength to get there.

So I left.

Chapter Zero

The morning buses fired up across the city. Early rising dog-walkers. Taxi cabs circling for one more fare. The indigo sky steeped in green, my legs sore, my head and feet aching, each car that passed me passed into my bones, each building I rolled beneath rubbed my heart raw. My mouth, the grid of intersections withered as spring's burgeoning leaves emerged from the gray limbs above. There was an hour available to me before Penny and Miller would wake up. I needed restoration, reconstitution, solace, the cold lake water, the answers of the sun.

Danny cycled through his Tai Chi positions in his usual spot where the sand butted the cement. A huge smile, he was always laughing pleasantly, friendly, and I did not know if he was terminally ill, the large growth under his skin where his neck joined his brain, but I assumed his clarity and kindness was forged by living so near to an end. He shouted so I could hear him, joyful about his question.

—How do you listen to your dreams when you don't go to sleep?

—I guess they'll have to wait for tomorrow.

—But now tomorrow is today.

He found himself very funny, his eyes beaming at me, his levity—I knew which direction he was headed.

Where the sand was wet from the water's reach, I took my clothes off and stepped into the lake, then plunged. The hum of the city vanished.

I needed a breath but before I emerged, I opened my eyes to study the green gray motion and dark texture of the waters. I swam to where I could just barely stand and popped my head up. The green horizon bent towards pink. The waters rose just a little and dropped. The highrises lurking over the lake were dark, a light turning on here and there, the balconies empty, the weathered 60s architecture out-of-place and therefore transportational, taking me to Miami, to Cuba, to the Baltic Sea. I am elsewhere. I am what I am not. Everything of this was me—the landscape, the scenery, the environment. I moved through myself. This night, these years—wherever elsewhere is—I will remain.

I had yearned for a sunrise and here it was, apologizing to the border of water and sky. The beginning, I said, of presence. I am sorry that I need you to be imaginable; I should let you rest.

I walked home but I didn't wake Michelle with a kiss until later, letting her know how much I loved her with a hug that set our souls aglow.

I sat in our wingback chair, and I cried, feeling relief from the low, loud sops and sniffling. I was right outside of Penny's room and accidentally woke her up. She got out of bed, opened her door and said *Hold you, Dad*. And she climbed into my arms and hugged me, falling back asleep as I closed my eyes.

Soon I heard Miller stirring, and I decided to take them to breakfast at The Coffee Shop. I left them in their PJs and put them in the burley to ride them up there, where Tammie and Jake were waiting.

—You remember Penny and Miller?

—Look at these beautiful kids. Take your usual table—the toys are there. We bought them hoping for grandchildren but no luck, right Jake?

—It all takes time.

—Our girls are still figuring out their passions while their eggs are shriveling up.

—Thanks for that image, Tammie.

—That's *tachlis* for you.

— These two have been begging for cinnamon rolls since last time, right kids? And I'll take a dark coffee.

—You betcha, little sweeties. The horses aren't racing this early, are they? Look at your eyes, you look horrible.

—What do you think kids, should we bet the ponies in Ireland?

173

—Dadda.

—The radio's not too loud for you?

—Loud. Dadda Mamma loud.

—Cacthing up on the news?

—Jake says it's all just noise. I know he's right but our people need to know the state of things.

—You can only control your awareness. Satchel knows. We sat down.

—Mama?

—Mama's still sleeping.

—Mama work mama?

—Good word, Miller. Yes, mama has work today.

There were times that I looked upon my kids as if they were magical creatures. Still connected to the cosmos, my reasoning went, and able to perceive things on a psychic level. They had powers, and I hugged them and gave them both kisses on their foreheads, as if I were rubbing a Buddha's belly for good luck.

—This is the good life, right kids? Café for breakfast with Dad. Jumping in the burley and riding over here. Let's do this a bunch this summer.

—Can we finish *Lord of the Rings*?

—Do you two want to?

—No, not really.

—Dadda no.

Though I knew my answer, out of habit I asked again. Wanting them, too much maybe, to have avenues into my struggles.

—Should Dadda be a lawyer?

—No Dadda. Mama.

—Penny, what do you think?

—Daddy, what's a lawyer?

—What do you think Dadda should do, Miller?

—Kook-kook.

—Make cookies.

—Ya. Kook-kook.

—We could open up a café and sell kook-kooks.

—Don't go putting us out of business. Here's your breakfast, kids.

—Thanks, Jake.

—Do you kids know your dad is a writer and your dad is a horseplayer?

—Ya. Ya.

—Our daddy reads books to us.

—Isn't that really neat—you all should be proud of him.

—Bon down?

—What's *bon down*?

—I think he means popcorn.

—Good memory, little guy. We pop the *bon down* later

when the kids are here studying.

—My dad should be a dad.

—I am always your dad, Penny.

—Tammie has your coffee at the counter there, Satchel.

—So, are you kids proud of me?

As soon as I asked, the anvil rose inside. My hot heart upon it, awaiting their blow. As I upon my father forged. To confer another form.

Miller grabbed Penny's cinnamon roll from her plate, and she screamed out as he threw it on the floor. They never answered.

—Jake, the radio! They just said it's coming. Here! Straight for Chicago.

—Tammie, what are you talking about?

—Jake—it just broke through the earth's atmosphere. Jake!

—Turn it up then, turn it up—I can't hear what they're saying.

—The girls! I'm going to call them.

—It's coming?

—Lock the doors. The doors, Jake!

—The city.

—Jake, not in front of the kids.

—Satchel, I think you need to get back on your bike.

—Tell Satchel his kids are going to be okay!

—Tammie wants me to tell you the kids are going to be okay.

—I will. Can we grab another cinnamon roll for the road?

KEVIN KILROY is a writer and a teacher living in Kansas City. His stories have been published by Akashic, Dispatches, Fact-Simile, Masque & Spectacle, Hot Whiskey, Poets & Artists, Sherlock Holmes & Philosophy and others. Kevin co-founded Black Lodge Press. He is the author of *The Escapees*, *Dead Ends* and *The Chicago Window* (Spuyten Duyvil).

Made in United States
Troutdale, OR
06/22/2024

20591484R00116